Pray for the Dead

Marc S. Blevins

Bloomington, IN Milton Keynes, UK

authorHOUSE®

AuthorHouse™
1663 Liberty Drive, Suite 200
Bloomington, IN 47403
www.authorhouse.com
Phone: 1-800-839-8640

AuthorHouse™ UK Ltd.
500 Avebury Boulevard
Central Milton Keynes, MK9 2BE
www.authorhouse.co.uk
Phone: 08001974150

First published by AuthorHouse 1/16/2007

ISBN: 978-1-4259-6306-4 (sc)
ISBN: 978-1-4259-6487-0 (hc)

Library of Congress Control Number: 2006911112

Printed in the United States of America
Bloomington, Indiana

This book is printed on acid-free paper.

Other books by Marc S. Blevins:

Hard Sell

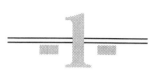

On the wall behind my desk hangs a framed photo of Jason Varitek shoving Alex Rodriguez in the face. I love that shot. Not because I harbor any particularly nasty feelings towards A-Rod. I love it because of the utter simplicity with which 'Tek says, "Enough." He's a stalwart, and a scrapper, and he goes to the wall for his teammates. And OK, it did make me giddy to see Rodriguez's way-too-pretty face get smothered in Varitek's glove. Bottom line: I hung that picture on my wall hoping it would make my clients think I'm tough.

It seemed to be working, too. The woman seated in front of me was blubbering so hard that her mascara would seep into my rug if she cried much longer. She was a small woman, with short, dark hair cut in an old-fashioned bob. She was very well dressed in a light-blue pants suit, her nails well manicured and polished, and if she spoke, I'm sure she would have been very well spoken.

But I didn't get to hear any words come out of her mouth, just the pleasure of a constant wail, which I was sure was confusing the hell out of any dog in a five-mile radius. Her sobbing began to subside into quiet whimpering, but tears still streamed down her face, and her shoulders shuddered in dry heaves that would eventually leave her exhausted.

To her left sat a large barrel-bodied man with small eyes and a thick mustache. He was round but didn't appear fat, and he sat with his feet planted firmly in front of him and his hand resting on the woman's left thigh. He was wearing a charcoal black suit, and even his belt buckle looked fastidiously polished.

I searched my desktop in vain for a box of Kleenex, but found nothing. Come to think of it, I wasn't sure if I had toilet paper in the bathroom. I sat back and let her finish. She wiped her eyes and looked at the floor. Worst-case scenario, I could always offer her my sleeve.

"You'll have to excuse my wife," the man said. "This is an extremely difficult time for us."

I nodded.

"You've heard of Jessica Stanchion?" he asked.

I nodded again.

"Teenager found dead on the beach in Newport," I said.

"We're her parents," the man said. "I'm Michael Stanchion, and this is my wife Vanessa."

Vanessa's whimpering had been reduced to short, quick intakes of breath. She looked blankly at the floor. Her husband's hand still rested lightly on her thigh.

"I'm sorry for your loss," I said.

"Thank you." He paused for a minute, looking at me. He took a deep breath. When he let it out, he continued. "Mr. Miller, our daughter was a good girl. She did not do drugs. I know, because I had her tested regularly. She didn't run with the wrong crowd; my wife and I kept very strict tabs on that. Our older son is serving a prison sentence for dealing heroin. We were not going to allow her to make the same mistakes as her brother."

He stopped. I had a feeling he wasn't finished, but there didn't seem to be anything for me to say at this point, so I kept quiet.

He looked off to the side for a minute, staring at nothing. When he had collected himself he returned his gaze to me and resumed his conversation.

"I have the utmost respect for our police department. There's no doubt in my mind that they will work as hard as they can to find whoever killed my daughter."

At this statement, a small moan issued forth from Mrs. Stanchion. Michael patted her thigh absentmindedly, something he'd probably been doing a lot the last few days.

"But the truth of the matter is the police cannot devote 100 percent of their time to this case. Other things will come up. Other things will need to be attended to."

I sat back in my chair and nodded again. So far I was doing a hell of a job holding up my end of the conversation.

"We wish to hire you, Mr. Miller," he said, "to find our daughter's killer."

"Sure," I said.

We sat there and looked at each other for a small amount of time.

"Not to be indelicate," I said, finally breaking the silence, "but there is the matter of my fee."

"Of course," Stanchion said, pulling his checkbook out from within his sports coat. "How much do you charge?"

I told him. He stopped midway through writing my name on the check and looked up at me.

"Man's gotta eat," I replied.

Stanchion cleared his throat quite loudly and finished writing the check. He handed it over the desk to me while giving me a hard stare.

"That should be enough for a retainer," he said in monotone. "And I'll expect a thoroughly itemized expense account when you are done."

"Certainly." I left the check sitting on my desktop.

Stanchion sat back and looked at me some more. His wife sniffled in the background. I waited patiently.

"Very well," he said finally, rising out of his chair. "We'll be in touch. I've notified the local police that I planned on hiring you. I've asked them to cooperate with you in any way necessary."

"I'm sure they're thrilled."

He lingered a moment longer than necessary, enjoying the dominance of standing over me, then turned, took his wife by the arm, and left.

I had just folded the check in half and placed it in my back pocket when Stanchion came back into my office. He sat down again in the same chair in front of my desk and leaned forward with his elbows on his knees.

"You want your check back?"

Stanchion took a breath in through his nose and let it out slowly.

"Find my daughter's killer, Mr. Miller." He looked at me steadily. "Find my daughter's killer and make sure he's dead."

"Might not be a he."

"Make sure he's dead."

He spoke slowly and deliberately. So did I.

"I don't do executions."

"I've heard differently. Do you have any children, Miller?"

"Not to my knowledge."

"You're not the only investigator in town, you know. I didn't have to come to you. Make sure he's dead. I'll double your retainer."

"Mike, this is Narragansett, Rhode Island. I am the only investigator in town. You don't want to hire me, fine. Tell me how to do my job, and I'll quit anyway."

Stanchion closed his eyes and hung his head.

"I'll find your daughter's killer, Mike."

He raised his head halfway.

"You better."

He turned to leave my office for the second time that day.

"You better, Miller. You charge more than a prostitute for your work."

"I date a hooker Mike," I said as he walked out. "Believe me. My rates are cheap."

My office was, in actuality, the remodeled spare bedroom in my house. And my house was, in actuality, the summer cottage I had rented last July. I turned off the various lights in the house, put on my jacket, exited through the door in the kitchen, and headed down the stairs. It was nearing the end of October in Rhode Island, which meant it was cool enough for a jacket, but not cold enough to have to warm up the car. I climbed into the Mustang, started it up, pulled out of the driveway, and headed over to Lil's.

After our stay last summer, we decided we actually liked Rhode Island enough to move here. What the hell. Our vacation had been such a pain in the ass, we figured if we lived here we might actually be able to enjoy it sometime. Everett sold our restaurant in Philadelphia and we split the profits four ways. Rhode Island real estate being what it is, especially by the beach, I took my share and bought the aforementioned cottage, using it as both a home and an office.

Lil, being who she is, maintained that there was no way in hell her home was going to be someplace where every fuckup in the state would be coming and going through her front door asking for help, or where inevitably someone would shoot at someone else, as bullet holes and bloodshed were no longer fashionable traits of home décor. Those being her words (verbatim), she took her share of the profits, as well as a portion of other monies she had amassed over the years, and bought the estate of the late Albert Crispin over on Harbor Island. Nobody tips the stripper who's worked the same club for the past fifteen years, a philosophy Lil ascribed to years back when she was actively hooking, and she had begun quietly investing her money, a practice that had obviously paid off big.

Everett and Nicole stayed in Virginia, where Everett started a securities consulting firm that became very lucrative very quickly. Nicole was steady at her job with the police as a forensic psychiatrist and was being utilized by the FBI more and more frequently.

So, to sum up, out of the four of us, the only one who didn't seem to be set for life, and had little to no cash on hand at all was, of course, me. Nobody seemed to mind.

I pulled up into the circular driveway and parked behind Lil's Jeep. The house hadn't changed much since Lil bought it. It still loomed over me as I walked to the front door. There was still a pool in back. And the house itself still contained more rooms than the Smithsonian. There was, however, no dead body waiting for me as I entered this time. Definitely an upgrade.

The sprawling staircase greeted me as I walked into the foyer. To my right, the dining room contained the new dining room set Lil had ordered last month. To the left was what Crispin had used as his office. Lil had filled half the bookcases with books, set up her computer on a mahogany desk in back, and then placed a full-sized TV on the opposite wall, surrounded by two armchairs and what I had deemed the most comfortable couch in the world.

She glanced up at me from the couch, where she was reading a magazine. She was barefoot and dressed simply in jeans and a T-shirt, which of course she wore with the grace of an upscale evening gown. Her red hair ran wildly down past her shoulders, and as she brushed it back with her fingers, the two bracelets I'd given her awhile back jingled down her arm. She stretched lazily and sat up. Her smile flashed a greeting at me, and her green eyes burned a warning. I'd dealt quite handily with the full repercussions of both, something that spoke of my toughness in ways that a poster of Jason Varitek never could.

"How was your day?" she murmured.

"Got hired," I said, hanging up my jacket.

"Has your client yelled at you yet?"

"Before he even finished signing the check."

Lil rearranged herself on the sofa, making room for me. I sat down next to her and put my feet up on the coffee table.

"He even went so far as to compare my rates to prostitution."

Lil leaned in and gave me a kiss on the cheek.

"I know what you charge," she said. "You don't even come close."

The TV sat in front of us with a screen so large that planes flying overhead were able to use it for their in-flight movies. Right now it was showing some sort of TV talk show where the hostess was taking turns crying and cheering along with her studio audience.

"See—" I said, pointing at the television. "This is why we don't live together."

"We don't live together," Lil said, getting up off the couch, "because if we did there's no way in hell we'd be able to stand each other. Now let's get something to eat."

She took my hand and walked with me into the kitchen. Lil's kitchen was the biggest room in the house. It wasn't that it held any more equipment than a normal kitchen; it had the traditional range-top stove, double-basin sink, dishwasher, and refrigerator. It was the fact that it ran the entire length of the back of the house and half the width. An island stood in the center of the room, around which were placed four bar stools, and a breakfast-nook table with six chairs sat in front of the sliding-glass door that opened to the back deck.

Lil had some shrimp and cocktail sauce in the fridge that she placed on the island, and then she placed three chicken breasts in the oven. She had a bottle of

Knob Creek bourbon, and I poured her a glass while I got myself a Jameson's over ice. I carried the drinks over while Lil chopped up some broccoli and placed it in a steamer on the back burner. When she finished, she joined me and sat opposite me at the island.

"So what's the case?" she asked, biting into a shrimp.

"Michael Stanchion asked me to look into the death of his daughter."

"Girl who was found dead on Newport Beach?"

I nodded and took a small sip of my drink. Gin and tonics were made for wiling away summer afternoons. Irish whiskey was perfect for enjoying an evening well into the night.

Lil picked a second shrimp up by the tail.

"What do you know so far?"

"Girl's dead. Father wants his daughter's murderer found and killed. Mother's a basket case."

"Acceptable reactions." Lil chewed her shrimp thoughtfully and dunked the second half in the cocktail sauce. "Will you kill the murderer when you find him?"

"Not really my place, is it babe?"

"I've seen you do it before." Lil crossed her legs and sipped her bourbon. "If you think it's the right thing to do, you will."

I shrugged.

"I don't know. Right now I need to find out about her. Who she is, where she came from. Hopefully from there I can pick up what happened." I paused and sipped my drink. "I'm a detective, sweetheart. I'm not a judge or an executioner."

Lil smiled a humorless smile.

"You're all three, Samuel, when it fits. Don't apologize for it. You are what you are. It's one of the reasons I love you."

We finished the shrimp and our drinks, and I brought some plates and silverware over to the breakfast table while Lil took the chicken breasts out of the oven. She had marinated them in a honey mustard sauce all day, and the smell permeated the kitchen. She emptied the broccoli into a bowl, I filled a glass pitcher with ice water, and the meal was complete.

One of the nicest things about Lil was that there were no false pretenses with her. She never made talk just to talk, and as such, there was nothing uncomfortable with eating our dinner in silence. When we finished, we rinsed the dishes, put everything in the dishwasher, and I took the trash outside. When I came back in, Lil had freshened our drinks, and we made our way into the solarium.

The solarium was a glass-enclosed porch located off the kitchen. It was the room where I had found the dead body of Albert Crispin. Lil had replaced the dead body and police chalk outlines with some comfortable deck furniture and a space heater to take the chill off during the fall evenings. She had also installed a set of speakers out there, and while she settled into her seat I put on a Buddy Guy album and let his voice growl out softly.

"You enjoying your foray into real estate?" I asked as I sat down in the chair beside her.

She took a sip of her bourbon and nodded. In early September Lil had acquired her real estate license. She'd shown a remarkable adeptness at it and had started turning profits very quickly. That didn't surprise me. I was curious as to whether she was seeing success because of genuine salesmanship or because she simply scared her clients into a purchase.

"I closed on three houses over the last two days. That's not bad. I don't know if I have the patience to do this over the long haul though."

"What do you mean?"

"I've got this one client, a real priss. I've shown her, like, fifteen houses, and none o' them are good enough. I think she honestly looks f'r something to bitch about in each o' them."

Whenever Lil got irritated, her Irish accent would become more and more pronounced in her conversation. It made me smile. I sat back and looked up at the sky through the glassed-in roof. It was a clear night. There wasn't a star in the sky.

"What are you going to do with her?"

"I'm showing her a property tomorrow. I told her if the house didn't appeal t'her I'd break her feckin' legs."

"You might think about printing that on your business cards."

She grinned at me over her glass.

"How do you plan on tackling the Stanchion case?"

"Jessica attended the high school here in Narragansett. Seems like a logical place to start. I'll stop by tomorrow, see if I can talk with a couple of her teachers."

"Probably be better off talking with some of the kids. They usually know more about what's going on than the teachers."

"You're probably right. Stanchion also said he alerted the local authorities that I'd be stumbling around."

"That means Lucille Simon."

"That means Lucille Simon," I repeated.

"Well won't she be thrilled to see you."

This time it was my turn to grin.

We finished our drinks in the solarium and watched the night sky for awhile. Then Lil turned off the space heater and I took our empty glasses back to the kitchen and rinsed them out. Lil moved about her house turning off the lights, and the two of us returned to her living room where she turned off the music and turned on her mammoth TV. She flipped around until she found a channel that was showing *L.A. Confidential*. I sat down on the couch, and she curled up next to me resting her head in my lap.

I was sure that somewhere across town the Stanchions were returning to a cold, empty, quiet home. They'd go through the motions of cooking and eating dinner, try to have a conversation, and then retire early to a fitful night's sleep.

They'd try not to listen for all the usual sounds of their daughter that they knew they wouldn't hear. They'd get up the next morning and eat some breakfast, go to work, and go through all the motions again. But it would seem cold and devoid of purpose.

I looked down at Lil and stroked her hair. She kissed my hand. She was warm and full of life. It didn't seem fair.

But it was right.

One year earlier

Tommy Bates had asked her out!

Jessica Stanchion ran in through her front door to share the news with her mother, but there was nobody home. A note on the kitchen table told her that her mother had driven to a charity function to help her father with his campaign. There was lasagna in the refrigerator for dinner; all she had to do was heat it up. Her mother promised that they'd try to be home by ten, but these things had a habit of running late, and every person her father met was one more potential vote he could get.

Jessica carried her books up to her bedroom and placed them on her desk. She lay down on her bed and breathed a happy sigh. Things were going so well! She had begged and begged and BEGGED her parents to let her go to public school like the other girls. Her parents had finally relented after she promised that her grades would not falter and that she would enroll in at least two after-school sports to keep up her resume for college. Thus she had started this year, her junior year, at Narragansett's high school.

She'd done everything she could to convince her father that it was a good idea, including pointing out that three of her four core courses her senior year could be used for college credit if she took the AP program and promising that she'd apply for early admission at two of the colleges he suggested.

But she knew what really twisted his arm was her suggestion that enrolling his daughter in public school would profess his value of the state's education system, thereby hopefully garnering support from the local unions in his bid for office. He liked that idea, and she was proud she had thought of it. She wanted to help her father win the election.

But more than anything she had wanted to go to public school like the other girls. And what a year this had been! She'd made friends and gone to basketball games and been invited places. Of course, her parents didn't always let her go—they had their rules—but she would see the other girls around town, and they would wave and say hello and she would wave back because they knew her and she knew them and they were friends. They would share music and talk about boys and help each other with their homework, the last of which Jessica was very good at. She studied very hard and was at the top of her class. She did not want her father to think that he made a bad decision and put her back in a private school. She played soccer in the fall and would start running track in the spring. If she worked very hard, her father would let her stay next year too.

And now Tommy Bates had asked her out. Tommy Bates! He was only the cutest boy in the whole school. And he was funny. And he started on the basketball team. And he had these blue blue eyes that made her melt every time he looked at her.

She lay back on her bed and closed her eyes. She pictured herself wearing his basketball jacket around school. Maybe they'd go to the prom. Maybe they'd even get their picture in the yearbook next year, with the title of "Cutest Couple" or something.

She giggled to herself. She knew she was being silly.

Tommy Bates Tommy Bates Tommy Bates

She was the happiest girl in the world.

Since we've entered the age of cable television, you can't fall asleep and wake up to the buzzing of the station identification anymore. Now, regardless of what time it is, you invariably wake up to some low-rent lousy-ass show that is playing on one of the 307 stations your cable network offers. I awoke on Lil's couch somewhere between two and three a.m., where I found the tail end of the movie *Diggstown* on the TV. This being the only movie with James Woods I ever enjoyed, I watched the last half hour and turned off the set.

The second floor of Lil's home was even larger than the first. I thought about joining her up in her bedroom, but the last time I tried to find my way around upstairs in the dark I got so lost I had to stay put for forty-five minutes until the sun came up. Learning from past mistakes, I pulled a blanket off the top of the couch and went back to sleep. When the sunlight finally bounced off the far wall through Lil's front window, it was six thirty in the morning, and I roused myself up.

I straightened up the living room and climbed the front stairs. Lil's upstairs housed four bedrooms, a study, two hall closets, a half bath in the hallway, and a full bath in the master bedroom. I'm sure there were more rooms hidden away somewhere—I just never bothered to look.

Lil's bedroom contained a deep, cedar-lined, walk-in closet, which, coupled with the other two hall closets, gave her storage for about 20 percent of her wardrobe. Ever generous, she allowed me to store a portion of my clothes in her home as well, which basically amounted to one pair of jeans and three T-shirts.

It wasn't cold enough yet to really crank up the heat, so Lil had left the door to her bedroom open. As I walked in, she was sound asleep under the covers. I entered the master bath, closed the door, and turned on the shower. I cleaned up, came back into the bedroom, and put on a fresh change of clothes.

"Are you leaving?"

Lil's voice murmured from the bed behind me. I closed the door to her closet and turned around. Her eyes were still shut. I bent down and kissed her forehead.

"I gotta go to work."

She smiled without opening her eyes.

"You gotta shave."

"Have to have something to look forward to," I said, and left.

I sat in my car at the top of Lil's driveway and called the Narragansett police station on my cell phone. As a rule I hate people who talk on their cell phones while they drive, and with my car being a standard, it's damn near impossible anyway. I got through to the front desk and asked for Lucille Simon. She was currently working her shift but was away from her desk at the moment. I hung up and called Everett at his office. I got his machine as well, but this time I left a message asking for any information involving the death of Jessica Stanchion. If there was anything worth knowing, Everett would dig it up by the end of the day. Don't misunderstand me. By no means do I think Everett's intelligence is any more credible than Ms. Simon's. But not being able to reach her by phone gave me an excuse to go visit her in person, which always proved to be infinitely more fun. I turned off the phone and tossed it onto the backseat. Then I started up the Mustang and coasted down Lil's driveway.

The sun came glancing off the water as I turned onto Ocean Drive. A few people jogged or walked their strollers along the sea wall next to the ocean, but the thinning crowd was one more piece of evidence that the summer was over and the cold season was on its way.

I pulled into the parking lot of the Narragansett police station. The station was still next to the library, and as I walked in, Lucille Simon's reaction to seeing me was still the same as well.

"The fuck do you want?" she asked as I sat down.

I placed a cup of Dunkin' Donuts coffee in front of her and sat back.

"Doesn't the coffee even get me a smile?"

"The coffee gets you jack shit. The three speeding tickets you asked me to fix last month—three, Sam, THREE—got me nothing but grief from my captain, and generally whenever I see you, you are nothing but a pain in the ass."

"But I'm fun to be with."

"Sam, I've been working the night shift for the last two weeks. I am not in a good mood. What do you want?"

Lucille's hair was pulled back tight in back of her head. She had on a cream-colored short-sleeved blouse, and while her desk blocked the rest of her, I guessed she was wearing a pair of simple dark slacks and matching shoes. Her nails were covered in a dark red polish and glinted in the light as she signed a seemingly endless pile of papers.

Over the summer we had cracked a blackmail scheme in Rhode Island. When we turned it over to Lucille, the press made her the poster child for talent on the police force, and her superiors promoted her to the rank of lieutenant. The promotion garnered her more respect, more money, and shittier hours. I was never sure if she was thankful or resentful towards me for that.

"You just need a good man, Lucille," I said. "Your mood would improve."

"I realize that. But instead I'm talking with you."

She stopped her flurry of activity for a moment, clasped her hands, and looked at me.

"Get to the point. I'm out of here in half an hour, and I desperately need some sleep."

"I've been hired by Michael Stanchion to look into the death of his daughter," I said. "I was hoping you could bring me up to speed."

"I heard you'd been hired," she replied. "Not much to tell. Girl was found dead on Newport Beach; gunshot wounds to the chest and head. Family lives here in town. Brother's in jail, father's been campaigning for governor for most of the last year."

"Think her death had something to do with Stanchion's campaign?"

"We are professional police officers, Sam. That thought did occur to us."

I nodded.

"Any leads?"

"Not really, not so far. We've looked into enemies Stanchion might have had, past associates of the brother, came up with zilch. He's all but disowned his son, and the rest of his life is spotless. Christ, the Brady Bunch could take lessons from his family."

"Didn't the mother date one of the sons on that show?"

"Aside from that."

"What about the girl herself?"

"Perfect. Absolutely perfect. Started attending school here in town last year. Straight A student. Before that, attended the state's premier private schools. Played soccer, ran track, a model student."

"As clean as the driven snow."

"Polly Pureheart."

We both looked at each other for a moment.

"This stinks," I said.

"Sure does."

"You got someone watching the house?"

"Of course. He leaves every morning early and gets home every evening after nine. He's an attorney in East Greenwich. By the afternoon he's out campaigning, going to lunches, functions, that sort of thing. She joins him for that, stays on his arm, plays the adoring wife. Up until then she runs around town doing errands. Nothing much. No one else goes in or out. They don't even have a maid."

"Imagine that."

"They don't have a clue who killed their daughter, Sam."

I stared at the wall behind Lucille. I thought about the two parents coming home to an empty house that probably seemed emptier each day.

"I should get going," I said, looking back at Lucille.

"Where are you going to start?"

"I figure I'll stop by the high school. I'll work the case from the other end, see what I can find out about her, and go from there."

"You're going to take on academia?"

"First time for everything."

She smiled.

It was about time.

"I was beginning to think you saved that smile for the mechanic you're dating, and only him."

"He's gone. I've moved on to a bartender."

"Can't go wrong with a bartender."

"We'll see. I'm going to enjoy hearing about you being pushed around by a bunch of kids."

"C'mon. You don't think my leather jacket makes me look tough?"

"Sure it does," she said. "But I've seen you in action."

She handed me a manila file folder.

"I had a copy of our case file made up for you. It's not much, but everything we've gotten so far is in there. Hope it helps."

Startled, I said thank you, stood up, and headed back out the way I had entered.

When I got to the door I asked, "How'd you know I was hired?"

"I gave Stanchion your number."

I turned back to look at her, but Lieutenant Lucille Simon was already re-immersed in the endless piles of paperwork on her desk.

One of the nicest things about Narragansett, Rhode Island, is the fact that everything is in close proximity to everything else, a trait indicative of the entire state. Case in point, the high school is two streets away from the police station. I could have easily walked, but I'd grabbed a Black Crowes CD and a live Chuck Berry album to play in the car before I left Lil's, and I figured that music would put me in a mood pleasant enough to deal with teenagers on a sunny morning. Besides, it was still early. I may have aged to my late thirties, but a strong part of me still wanted to spend as little time in school as possible.

I drove around town and listened to five songs off the second album, letting the music grind out of the speakers. Life is all about rhythm. If you find music that mirrors yours, you're all set. I parked at the sea wall and watched the sun splash itself across the street. I flipped through the morning's paper and ended up reading more than I intended. By quarter to nine I figured the school day was underway enough that I could stop by and talk with somebody moderately awake. I put the car in gear, turned right at the granite well in the middle of the street, and climbed the two blocks to the high school.

The high school building was set back from the road and encircled by a thin forest of trees, giving the feeling of separation from the rest of the world so that one could focus on one's studies. It was a feeling I got at almost any school.

I was greeted by a soccer field and a football field as I made my way down the driveway and finally ended at a small parking lot in front of the school. I parked in a visitor's space, turned off the car, and walked to the main entrance. Having spent the greater portion of my life in the so-called "real world," my memories of school seemed blurry and distant. Still, I tried to remember some sort of school etiquette and removed my sunglasses as I entered the building.

A plush red carpet blanketed the atrium floor just beyond the main doors. In front of me was a trophy case memorializing local heroes past and present. Offices to the right and left of me housed professional-looking adults working at their desks, talking with the occasional student who meandered in. Off in the distance I saw the sign for the library entrance. In the distance phones rang and voices spoke softly. I didn't see many students, which meant that either classes were in session or "Bunk Day" had risen to entirely new heights.

Being a trained detective, I spotted the sign on the frosted glass stating, "All Visitors Must Report to the Main Office," and entered the door on my left. It was the most headway I'd made so far, but Stanchion had paid in advance. He deserved to get his money's worth for the day.

An older woman with short, white hair sat behind the desk in the main office. A brown wool sweater was draped over her shoulders, and glasses hung from her neck on a gold chain. She had a calm demeanor about her, that of someone who had witnessed the cycle of adolescence numerous times and was no longer fazed by anything that came through her door. She smiled at me as I came in and rested her hands on the desk in front of her.

"Good morning," she said. "May I help you?"

I smiled back at her.

"I'm sure you can," I said. "My name's Samuel Miller."

I handed her my card. She read it and then looked at me, giving me a conspiratorial wink along with her smile.

"A private investigator. Oh my. Am I in trouble?"

"Not yet," I laughed. "If I searched around would I dig up something criminal on you?"

"More than you could handle. May I ask why a private detective is visiting our cozy little high school?"

"I'm looking into the death of Jessica Stanchion."

She shook her head sadly and cast her eyes downward.

"That poor girl. Such a lovely girl. Such a shame." She reached out absentmindedly and patted my hand. "The police were here last week. I'll go get the principal. He talked with them already."

She walked off down a side corridor and returned momentarily with a tall man dressed in a black suit. She kept her hand on his arm in a motherly fashion and guided him over to me.

"This is Donald Rivers, our principal. Don, this handsome young man is a private investigator. He's here about Jessica."

Donald Rivers extended his hand and I shook it. He had a firm, no-nonsense handshake, a high forehead, thick, dark hair, and broad shoulders. He looked like he could be a linebacker in the NFL. His eyes met mine, gave me the once-over, and then looked past me in a tired but patient manner. I'm sure I was supposed to be intimidated.

"I'm a bit confused as to how I can help you, Mr.—?"

"Miller," I said, trying not to grin. "Samuel Miller."

James Bond has nothing on me.

"Yes, Mr. Miller. I've already spoken with the police. I'm afraid I don't see how I can be of any more useful service to you."

"I've been asked by the Stanchion family to look into the case. I'm hoping to learn a little about Jessica and see if that might lead me anywhere."

"Yes, very good, very good. Well, she was a wonderful girl. Bright girl. Pretty girl. Damn shame what happened."

"So I've heard. Is there anyone you could direct me to who might offer a more, ah, descriptive view of her?"

I'm pretty sure I saw the secretary's eyes light up, if only for a second.

Rivers' brow furrowed in deep concentration for a moment, and then he replied with, "You might check with Valerie Robinson. She's the head of our guidance department. She could probably help you out."

"Thanks," I said. "I think I'll do that."

"No problem, no problem." He took my hand and pumped it vigorously twice. "Anything I can do. Glad I could help. If I can help you again in the future, don't hesitate to call."

He turned and went back down the corridor, presumably to his office where a host of educational issues awaited. I looked back over at the secretary. She tried very hard to suppress a laugh. She almost succeeded.

"The guidance department is right across our foyer," she said, pointing out the door. A phone rang behind her. "You'll have to excuse me. Duty calls."

I left the office. As I walked back across the foyer, I caught the beginning of her phone conversation. She was explaining to a parent, in an extremely patient manner, that if the student was too sick to attend school, the student could not play in tonight's football game, even though a miracle recovery had occurred before noon.

The door to the guidance office was open, and as I entered I was greeted by a tall, dark-skinned woman in a white top and red skirt. She wore heels, but even without them she'd still tower a good two inches over me. Her blue eyes smiled at me from within her obsidian skin, and her braided hair was tied back and fell almost to her waist.

"I'm looking for Valerie Robinson, please."

"That would be me," she said, shifting a stack of papers to her left arm and extending her right hand. "Walk me to my office and I'll give you five minutes. I have a student coming down to see me."

Her office was the third room of four and was not very large. Valerie took a seat at her desk, and I sat down in one of the two remaining seats against the wall. Valerie's office contained a computer, a bookcase stacked with various books and binders, and a stand in the corner that held various pamphlets denoting the benefits of going to college, getting a job, or joining the service. I wondered if she had access to my permanent record. I didn't think it would be very impressive. I wasn't sure my present-day credentials were all that impressive.

"Now," she said, turning to look at me while crossing her legs, "what can I do for you?"

I explained my reason for the visit, handing her my card as well.

"I just met with your principal," I finished up, "but his recollection of Jessica seems to be from a yearbook photo."

"That sounds like Donald," she frowned. "If Jessica hadn't been killed I doubt he'd even know who she was."

"Not exactly the most admirable quality in a high school principal."

"Donald's not the most admirable principal. What can I do for you?"

"Anything you can tell me about Jessica would be helpful," I said. "Even if it seems irrelevant. I'm trying to put together a picture of this girl."

"Jessica was a wonderful girl. Excellent student, made honors every quarter. She was a very hard worker and excelled in academics. I know she played soccer..."

Valerie pulled one of the binders off the shelves and leafed through it. The binder was large enough to register as carry-on luggage on an airline flight. She had six of them.

"Here it is. She played soccer and ran track."

Valerie turned the binder around and handed it to me. I flipped through Jessica's transcripts. French V. Calculus. Advanced Physics. College-level English. Straight A's in all of them. Her yearbook photo stared back at me off the page. She was a stunning girl with long curly blond hair. Her smile beamed with warmth and innocence.

This sucked.

"Is there anything you could tell me about her personally?" I asked as I closed the binder and gave it back to her. "Who she dated, who her friends were, anybody she didn't get along with?"

"There wasn't anyone she didn't get along with," Valerie said, smiling and shaking her head. "She was extremely sweet and actually quite shy. She transferred here at the start of last year. Up until then she attended Queens Academy, a very rigorous, very prestigious private school in Providence. I know she was excited to attend public school, and she seemed to acclimate herself quite well. You know how teenagers can be. Acceptance is everything. She seemed to fit in pretty easily here."

The bell rang. Within seconds the halls were brimming with noise as students filed out of one class and tried to catch up on all the worldly gossip before having their attention diverted back to education.

Valerie stood up. "I'm sorry, Mr. Miller, but that's all the time I can spare. I have thirteen students I'm supposed to meet with before the end of the period."

"Did she have a boyfriend?" I asked as I stood.

"I think she dated Tommy Bates. He's one of our basketball stars. Girls follow him around from class to class hoping to carry his books." She smiled. "Y'know, it used to be the other way around."

"Basketball season hasn't started yet, right?"

"No, but the coach lets them scrimmage in the gym after school. Tommy's usually there with some of the other boys for an hour or two."

A voice crackled over the intercom. "Mrs. Robinson, Jeremy Wise is here to see you."

"I have to go," she said. "That's my first student."

"Think anybody would mind if I stopped by the gym after school and talked to Tommy?"

"There's probably a delineated protocol somewhere that asks you to register as a visitor and then make sure some sort of school official is present while you interview a student. But," she said as she looked me straight in the eye, "I've learned that it's much easier to get forgiveness than it is to get permission."

She held the door open for me as I left.

Michael Stanchion, one year earlier

Michael Stanchion admired himself in the mirror.

His hair was neatly combed; the salt-and-pepper look had received many compliments all evening. His mustache was neatly trimmed, his suit freshly pressed and made to order. He looked and felt at the top of his game. How could you not enjoy this?

The campaign was going better than he had anticipated. He had called in as many favors as he could from his position as an attorney, and every one of them had paid off. He was welcomed with a smile everywhere he went. People greeted him as he walked in the door, looked for him as he walked down the street. He didn't seek people out; people came to him. They came to him. His friends and former clients began a word-of-mouth campaign for him, and overnight his reputation had ballooned in stature. If people didn't know him, they felt like they should and made an effort to spend time with him at any event he attended.

People came to him.

It was intoxicating, really. Enjoyable, but not overwhelming. As a youth, Michael had spent summers surfing the waves of Matunuck. He remembered the exhilaration of mastering the waves and riding them to the shore on his board.

Owning the ocean instead of the ocean owning him. He tamed the waves and watched while others were buffeted about by them, subject to the whims of the ocean. Not him. He read the waves and used them to steer him home. He was in charge.

It was the same thing now. Different environment, same feeling. Power. When it came down to it, that's what it was all about, what it had always been about. And it was coming to him almost unbelievably easy.

But it was believable.

He had to remind himself of that. Everything that was coming to him he had worked for. He had earned. He deserved.

And it wasn't just him either. His wife would reap the benefits. So would his daughter. His son, well, there was only so much that could be done there. But a line had to be drawn somewhere; losses had to be cut. That couldn't be helped.

Michael Stanchion stepped out of the restroom and back into the ballroom. He surveyed his surroundings. This event had been a good one. Hell, they were all good lately. Elegant setting, well attended, and by some of the more prominent people in the region.

Two very well-dressed and very pretty young women from the State House walked by. He smiled at them. They smiled back. That was happening a lot lately. Well why shouldn't it? With the position comes power, and with power comes perks. He'd have to start taking advantage of some of those perks.

He'd earned them.

He deserved them.

He scanned the room and found his wife. She was speaking with the secretary of state and her husband. He chuckled to himself. She really did enjoy these outings. Perhaps he could create some position for her once he was elected. Give her something to do, help her feel fulfilled. Give him more time to pursue his interests as well.

The senator from Massachusetts entered the room. Michael crossed the floor to shake his hand.

It never hurt to start laying the groundwork for future relationships.

I walked back across the parking lot to my car. The wind scattered some leaves through the air and blew a crumpled Doritos bag across my feet. I thought about what I had learned. Jessica Stanchion didn't have an enemy in the world, the principal didn't have a clue, and the guidance counselor didn't have enough time in the day to accomplish what she wanted. All in all, I didn't like school any more than I had when I had entered.

I put my hands in my pockets and leaned against my car, staring out over the football field. Normally in murder cases, the first suspect is the victim's spouse. Jessica Stanchion's being quite single at the age of seventeen would switch the focus over to boyfriend Tommy Bates, Narragansett's resident hoops star. But why in hell would a teenager kill his girlfriend? She wouldn't put out? According to Valerie, Tommy has a fan club that follows him around on an hourly basis. Scoring a date didn't seem like a problem for him.

Did Jessica give Tommy some unwanted news? Maybe she did come across for him and became pregnant as a result. Hopefully an autopsy would reveal that, but maybe the medical examiner stopped with the gunshot wounds. Being a father might slow down Tommy's efforts to pursue a state title. But enough to make homicide seem appealing? Believable, but not likely.

Something was missing. I didn't have a complete picture.

There was a scoreboard raised behind one of the goalposts, and a gravel track encircled the football field. My eyes passed back over the field, and I saw what appeared to be cigarette smoke coming from the bleachers.

Well it was about time.

Principals and guidance counselors were out of my league. Delinquents I could deal with.

I walked down the hill towards the football field and climbed into the bleachers. There were three of them, sitting together, smoking. One was a very large boy; the other two were short and thin. Large Boy wore a big Green Bay Packers jacket, a blue scarf, and the type of cap I never knew the name for and forever described as an Irish drinking cap. One of the other boys had a crew cut and wore a green fisherman's sweater and corduroy pants. The third boy had long dirty hair that hung in his face. He was dressed in blue jeans, work boots, and an oversized, thermal-lined flannel shirt. I walked up the bleacher steps and sat down next to them.

"Good morning."

The three of them stared at me in silence. The skinny kid with long hair took one last drag on his cigarette and stared at me through the smoke. He ground his cigarette under his boot and looked back at me.

"Mornin'. Who are you?"

"My name's Samuel Miller."

I handed each of them a card. They took their time reading them.

"Private detective?" Long Hair said. "Like in the movies, man?"

"You got a gun?" Crew Cut asked. He talked out of the side of his mouth even when he looked straight at you.

I held my jacket open to show them my shoulder rig.

"Shit, man," Long Hair laughed, pointing, "That's the shit, that is. Guy comes to school packing a fucking gun. That's all right."

"I dunno," Crew Cut said, lighting another cigarette. "My dad's is bigger."

Thank the Almighty no one had said that statement to me before.

"You gonna turn us in for smokin'?" Large Boy asked, staring out at the field.

"No, I'm not gonna turn you in for smoking. I'm investigating the death of Jessica Stanchion."

"Jessica," Long Hair said, nodding approval.

"Shot in the head," Crew Cut said, cocking his thumb and pointing his finger at his head. "Bang."

"Can you tell me anything about Miss Stanchion?" I asked.

"Hottie."

"Hottie."

"Definite hottie."

They all seemed to be in agreement.

"Too bad she's dead," mused Crew Cut.

"Yeah," Long Hair agreed. "You can't nail a corpse. And she was—"

"Don't be an asshole," I interrupted. "I haven't decided I don't like you yet."

"Sorry man, I just—"

"I have a gun."

He shut up.

"How about Tommy Bates?" I probed.

"Tommy," Long Hair smiled. "Tom-me." He laughed to himself, all fear gone again. "Tommy's the man. He gets any piece of ass he wants. Any piece."

"Girls like Tommy?" I asked.

"Yeah," Crew Cut nodded. "The girls like Tommy."

Large Boy continued to smoke and stare out at the grass.

"The girls lo-ove Tommy," Long Hair said, gesticulating with his hands. "Broads, books, and basketball. That's Tommy's motto. Broads, books, and basketball."

He laughed out loud, apparently satisfied with his own joke. I didn't get it.

"Did Jessica like Tommy?"

"They liked each other," answered Crew Cut. "They were steady for awhile. Steady right up until she died." He thought about what he said and looked at me again. "Tommy didn't kill her though, man."

"I didn't say he did. You think of any reason why someone would want Jessica dead?"

"No, man," Crew Cut said. "She was all right. I don't know why someone shot her."

Long Hair shook his head. Large Boy continued to stare out at the field.

"If you think of anything, give me a call."

I stood up.

"You gonna turn us in?" Large Boy asked.

"No," I said, and walked down the bleacher steps.

I climbed back up the hill to my car. The only thing I had learned since my arrival was that Tommy Bates was apparently the school stud. It wasn't much, but it was more than I had when I started. I unlocked my door and started up the car. As a reward for my efforts I put a BossTones disc in the CD player. Then I drove out of the parking lot.

Tommy wouldn't be in the gym until after school at roughly two thirty. I had a lot of time to kill and not a whole hell of a lot to do. When all else fails, I say eat. I drove my car down towards a bar that was across from the beach in the southern part of town. The bar was typically frequented by college students and wouldn't be all that busy at this time of day.

There were pockets of neighborhoods located around Narragansett where the students from URI would rent homes for the year. As the college was located in the next town over, living off-campus was typically referred to as living "down the line." Clusters of homes catering to college students would spring up in various parts of town, thus sequestering them into various areas of Narragansett.

Sonny's was a bar that happened to be located within walking distance of one of these pockets and hence had come to be known as a down-the-line bar. This basically meant it was busy Wednesday night through Saturday night from ten to one and pretty much dead the rest of the time. It wasn't because the food wasn't good; it was because the college kids scared people.

I parked the car and walked up the stairs to the second floor. In a few weeks the deck would be closed for the winter, and I wanted to get as much use out of it as I could before they locked it up. Plastic sheeting had been put up to keep the chill off the outer deck, and the inside bar was still warm. I walked into the empty room and took a seat at the empty bar.

"Twenty bucks says you're my only customer today," Danielle called out as she walked in from the kitchen carrying two cases of beer. "I don't think anyone else even knows we open before nine p.m."

Danielle set the two cases down on the coolers behind the bar. She had dark, dark hair, which she had braided in pigtails. She wore a white T-shirt with the Harley-Davidson logo, a short, ruffled jean skirt, and motorcycle boots. She smiled at me and opened the cases.

"You're out of beer already?" I asked as she began stacking bottles into the coolers.

"Shoulda been done last night. Assholes don't know how to close a goddamn bar. You want a gin and tonic?"

"Dani, it's not even eleven."

"That's why I didn't offer whiskey."

"I'll settle for water and a menu, sweetheart. Thanks."

"You gettin' to be a puss in your old age, Sammy," she grinned and threw a menu in front of me.

"You haven't even known me six months. How's school?"

"Passing engineering, acing calculus, flunking literature. Really Sam, when am I going to need to be able to quote fucking nineteenth-century poetry? Bunch of dead gay pricks blowing my GPA."

"Especially when you're so eloquent yourself."

She flipped me off and placed my water in front of me.

The bar was named Sonny's, but no one knew of any Sonny who had ever worked there, let alone owned it. The current owner was a man named Billy Riel. Billy was a good guy, much nicer than he should be, mostly because he had people like Danielle around to enforce the rules.

"You should ask Billy to give you a couple of night shifts. I understand this day shift is very exciting, but you might actually make money at night."

"I work four nights, wiseass. Carmine called in sick again. I'm covering his shift."

"That's nice of you."

Dani finished stocking the beer coolers and flattened down the cardboard boxes.

"He's called in sick three times in the last six weeks. He was stupid enough to call in this morning, after he sat on his ass and drank Guinness here all last night." She tossed the flattened boxes in the far corner of the room. "I fired him this morning over the phone."

"Fired?"

"More like threatened. I told him if he ever showed his little dick face in here again, I would personally make sure that he would leave as even more of a woman than he was when he came in."

"Verse like that from you, and you're failing poetry. It doesn't make sense."

"You think?" She came around to the front of the bar and sat down next to me. She picked up the newspaper I had brought in and started leafing through it.

"Aren't you supposed to take my order?"

"You get hungry, tell me what you want. I'll go tell the cook."

"That sounds fair."

We sat there for the better part of an hour. We read the paper and shared a club sandwich.

It was an excellent break in the day.

The world is run by secretaries, nurses, and security guards. Ask anybody. If they have a shred of common sense, they'll agree. My interaction earlier at the school had only served to reinforce my beliefs.

I passed a couple of kids skipping out early as I drove down the driveway to the school and parked the Mustang back in a visitor's slot. I crossed over to the entrance and made my way back into the principal's office for the second time that day. It was starting to feel like I really was back in school.

The secretary looked up from her typewriter and smiled broadly at me.

"Back again?"

"I couldn't keep away," I said.

"I'll bet."

The sunlight reflected off the windowpane in back of her and actually formed a halo above her white hair. Swear to God.

"What can I do for you this time?" she asked.

"I was wondering if there was a copy of a yearbook available. I was hoping to take a look at it and see if I could get a sense of Jessica's high school life through pictures."

It sounded like even more of a long shot saying it out loud.

"The yearbooks are in the library," she said, coming around her desk. "I'll take you there myself."

She didn't move particularly fast, but who in their right mind was going to tell a woman in her upper sixties to step on it? She came around and took my arm, just as she had with the principal earlier this morning, more for effect than for balance. She didn't come up taller than my chest and had to reach up to hold onto my arm, but I'll be damned if she planned on letting go. Ah, if she were only forty years younger.

The library was literally right around the corner from the office and was actually quite large for a school library. Tables and chairs ran the length of the room, including the far section, which was raised up on a four-step loft. Bookcases lined the walls, and all of them looked to be fully stocked. The secretary led me around the librarian's desk and through a door to a back office. Catalogues, manuals, and magazines were stacked in various piles, and four TV/VCR stands were pushed off to the side.

"Here we are," the secretary said, letting go of me and walking over to one of the shelves. She pulled down one of the books. "This is last year's yearbook."

"Are you going to tell me your name, or are you going to make me ask you for your phone number?" I asked.

"My, my. Handsome and sweet. What a nice young man. My name's Doreen."

"Thank you for your help, Doreen," I said.

"Such a gentleman. It was my pleasure."

She walked out the door and back towards the office. I found a table in the far corner of the library and scanned the pages of the yearbook. Jessica's yearbook shot was the same one in Valerie's folder, and I found her in the soccer team shot as well.

Nobody had exaggerated about Jessica Stanchion. She was a very pretty girl. And happy too. There weren't many shots of her in the yearbook, but in the few there were, her smile beamed out at you from the page. I began to understand what Valerie had meant about acceptance. Jessica was never in the center of the action in any of the pictures, which was surprising given the way everyone had spoken of her. But the look in her eyes and the smile on her face were unmistakable. She was simply happy to be part of the group. She was just happy to be in on the fun.

Tommy Bates was a whole other story. Tommy Bates was the group. You couldn't find three pages in a row where Tommy wasn't featured in at least one photo. Sitting in the middle of the National Honor Society. Working with the elderly in the Community Outreach program. Smacking the shit out of a piñata at the Spanish Club Christmas party. Being crowned king at the junior prom.

I checked the cover a second time to make sure it wasn't entitled the *Tommy Bates Yearbook.*

The basketball section looked as if Tommy had hired his own personal photographer. In three pages, Tommy was in seven photos. He was captain his junior year, led his team in rebounds, and had been elected All-State in both his sophomore and junior year.

His pictures showed him to be exactly what you would expect him to be: charming, ruggedly handsome, athletic, popular, confident, and cocky. But how could you not be when the rest of the school celebrated you for those very qualities?

"I'm guessing you're not a new student."

The voice was unmistakably feminine, and definitely adult. I looked up from my seat to find a young, professional, blond-haired woman smiling down at me. Her hair was pulled back in a short ponytail, her deep-blue eyes looked straight at me, and her smile came easy. She wore a blue silk blouse and a short, flowered skirt that ended a little bit above the knee. This, in turn, gave me ample opportunity to notice her legs, which was turning out to be the smartest thing I'd done all day.

"Are you looking at my legs?" she asked, still smiling.

"Checking out your shoes," I said, turning to look up at her face.

"Really. Could you tell me what color my shoes are?"

"Don't confuse me."

She pulled out a chair and joined me at the table. I gave her one of my cards, and even though I assumed she could read, told her my name anyway.

"A private detective," she said. "Mm."

Not the best reaction I'd received so far.

"And you would be in my library because....?"

"So you would be the librarian," I said.

"Brilliant detective."

"Well I'm getting paid. I have to be."

She laughed. It was a start.

"I'm looking into the death of Jessica Stanchion." I was getting tired of repeatedly explaining myself. Tomorrow I'd just start passing out flyers. "I was hoping to familiarize myself with some names and faces through your yearbook. Try and get a sense of what her life was like while she was here."

The librarian pulled the yearbook over.

"You're looking at the basketball team."

"Yeah, I heard she dated Tommy Bates. Do you know him?"

"Tommy? It's a small school. It's impossible not to know Tommy. I see most of the kids in here on a regular basis. Tommy's in here more than most, always with a group, always cutting up. Life of the party, y'know? Good kid."

"How'd he act with Jessica?"

"Tom? I never saw them together."

"Didn't they date each other?"

"I dunno." She looked over the basketball photos. "It's so hard to tell these days, you know? I don't know if anyone even goes steady anymore." She smiled. "Including me for that matter."

I smiled back. "Do you remember anything about Jessica?"

"She was quiet. Aloof. Nice enough, but she kept to herself."

The bell rang. Students began gathering their materials and walking out the door as others started coming in.

"I've got to go man the desk," she said, closing the yearbook and drawing it towards her. "One more period to go."

"If you think of anything, Miss...."

"Hurdtz. Gloria Hurdtz. I have your number." She held up the card. "If anything comes up I'll give you a call."

She smiled one more time, briefly, and turned and walked away, hugging the yearbook close to her chest. I got up and walked to the other end of the library. I'd noticed a map of the school hanging on the wall when I came in and took a moment now to check out the layout of the school. Valerie said Tommy would probably be in the gym after school. I looked at the map. The gym was on the other end of the school. There was a parking lot outside the gym. Easy. I turned around, gave a quick wave to Gloria Hurdtz, who looked up briefly, and walked out.

The sun was shining brightly as I walked back to my car. It was one of those days in October that tease you as the rays cut through the chill for a few condensed hours, reminding you of the warmth of summer and the hope for spring. For a minute I was envious of the students at the school. For many of them, their work day was basically over. The rest of the day consisted of pickup games, cheering on the football team, or trying to sneak your boyfriend into the house while Mom was still at work. I thought about where my life had gone since high school. Then I thought about calculus homework. I wasn't that jealous anymore.

I drove around to the back of the school and searched for a parking spot. Either the lot was smaller than it seemed or everyone and their brother at the school had a vehicle, because the place was packed. Luckily I found a spot that read "Reserved for Principal" that was empty, so I pulled right in.

Before the advent of cell phones, this would have been a perfect opportunity to kick back with a newspaper or magazine, killing time until the person you were waiting for, in this case Tommy Bates, made himself available. Now that virtually everyone and his dog has a cell phone, communication with other people is accessible twenty-four hours a day, which makes it that much harder, for private detectives anyway, to spend good quality time goofing off. Fortunately for me, when I checked my cell phone it read "No New Messages," which meant I was fully able to kick back. Last period of the day at school, and I was sitting outside of class doing absolutely nothing. It's good to remember your roots.

Of course, I had already finished reading the paper with Danielle, and I didn't have any magazines in the car, so I spent the next forty-five minutes in agonizing boredom, staring out the windshield of my car and watching the few stragglers who snuck out of class early. These people who say they go to the park to "people-watch" are out of their minds.

Finally the bell rang, and a mass exodus of students exploded from the building. It was pandemonium in the parking lot, and then a mass traffic jam converged out of nowhere as twelve buses and a hundred cars tried to exit the school simultaneously. This apparently was a well-oiled practice, because within ten minutes the parking lot was empty and peace had returned to the school.

I took this as my cue and got out of my car and walked to the back entrance. Two girls were leaving as I arrived, and they politely held the door open for me. I walked through the vestibule to the inner hallway and then in through the gymnasium doors on the right. The gym was empty and almost lonely, with the bleachers pushed against the walls and three kids dribbling a basketball between them, the ball and their shouts echoing through the vacant space. I suspected that when it was full with engaged teams and roaring fans, the gym, as all gyms do, became an entirely different animal. Right now, however, it was just a space for kids to wile away their spare time.

Tommy Bates walked out of what I presumed to be the locker room and strode over to join the other kids on the court. He looked just like his yearbook picture, sandy brown hair, rugged good looks, developing muscle, and a cocky strut to complete the picture. I walked across the gym floor to intercept him before he reached his teammates.

"Tommy Bates?"

He turned when I called, with a look of mild curiosity at who would be disturbing him in his castle.

"Yeah."

"My name's Samuel Miller," I said, extending my hand. "I was wondering if I could steal a couple minutes of your time."

"You from the paper?"

How nice it must be to be so ignorant that you think the entire world revolves around your own accomplishments.

"Not exactly." I handed him a card. I'd given out more today than in the entire month of August. "I'd like to talk with you about Jessica Stanchion."

He looked at the card and then back at me. The realization that this interview had nothing to do with the home opener began to dawn on him.

"Uh-uh. I already did this with the police. They said I didn't have to talk with them anymore."

"Humor me."

"Oh, c'mon man, what? Yes, we dated. Yes, we were a couple. No, I didn't notice her acting any differently. No, I don't know why anyone would want her dead. And no, I didn't kill her. Man, I wasn't even with her that night. Anything else?"

"Yeah. You rehearse all those answers before or after your first round of questioning with the police?"

He shut his mouth, took a step back, and eyed me like he was taking measure of me. Then he started again. "Tough guy. Tooooough guy. What, you think I did it? You want to take me down to the station for an interrogation?" He took his time speaking, overenunciating each syllable in "interrogation." "Take me down to the station." He held his arms out in front of him like he was about to be handcuffed. "Pretty please. Pretty please take me down to the station."

He wasn't shouting, but he was posturing enough that the other three boys at the end of the gym had stopped shooting the ball around and were now staring at the two of us. I waited until he was finished.

"You think of anything that might be useful, Tom, give me a call."

"Don't waste my time." He made a dismissive gesture, and walked towards the other boys, calling for the ball. They tossed it out to him, and, just to assert the fact that I was indeed on his turf, he took a shot and sunk a three-pointer. Swish. Nothing but net. They started to scrimmage, and for all they cared, I was no longer even in the room.

A good psychiatrist would probably point out Tommy's quick agitation, brash defensiveness, and abrasive challenge of authority. I'm not a shrink. I'm a detective. I just thought he was a prick.

I sat in my car and looked through the file Lieutenant Simon had given me on the Stanchion case. The only mention it had of Tommy was that he'd been questioned by the police the afternoon Jessica's body had been found. He said he hadn't gone out the night before. His parents had vouched for him. Nowhere in the report did it mention he was an asshole.

Shit, I was learning more on this case than the police were.

I left the school and drove around town a bit, letting my mind wander. From all accounts, Jessica was a sweetheart, a quiet, pleasant girl. Everybody except the librarian noted that Tommy and she dated, and Tommy changed the subject abruptly upon being questioned about her. On paper, he looked like the perfect suspect. Christ, after meeting him, I wanted it to be him. But again, where was the motive? Didn't seem like he stood to gain anything with Jessica dead.

I drove towards the north end of town, took a right down a side street, and drove slowly past the Stanchion's home. I don't know what type of revelation I hoped to get by driving by their house, but I slowed enough to take a look at where they lived. Their house was modest in size, set back a bit from the stone wall that separated their front yard from the road.

The driveway was an asphalt circle with a flower garden centered directly in the middle. In the driveway were three cars: a black four-door Lincoln Continental, a Jaguar convertible, and an all-wheel-drive Subaru station wagon. My guess was that the Jag belonged to Michael Stanchion, and the Subaru was for the missus, to help her through the rough New England winters. The sedan probably belonged to some political figure come to discuss Stanchion's political strategies over tea. There was nothing to learn here, especially if Mike was actively engaged in his future at the moment. I turned the car around and headed back towards the center of town.

I picked up a grinder at a local deli and parked in the town beach parking lot to eat it. The parking lot was getting emptier with each passing day, as more and more residents accepted the fact that fall was here and winter was coming and turned their thoughts away from the beach and towards other more-seasonal activities. The only diehards who showed up on a regular basis were the surfers, Narragansett's answer to the Viking mentality. They surfed on a daily basis religiously, and the worse the weather, the longer they stayed.

I watched them assemble on the beach, donning their wet suits and carrying their boards. Surfers were truly people of passion. If you spoke to them, you came away with the feeling that surfing was really their job, and anything they did with the other hours of their day was just a hobby.

I tried it once over the summer. One of the locals had said he'd teach me, and we got to the beach early in the morning, a short board for him and a long board for me. We paddled out a ways, turned the boards around, and sat upright on them, bobbing in the water. We continued to bob for the next eighty minutes, at which point I turned to my friend and asked him what we were supposed to do next. He looked over at me in the austere sunlight and replied, "Dude, we wait for the perfect wave." As life changing as that experience had the potential to be, I found other ways to occupy my time from that day forward.

I finished my sandwich, tossed the trash in the proper receptacle, said hello to a few of the people milling about, and got back in my car. When all else fails, start over, so I called it quits on the case for the day and headed over to the gym. If the mind's not working, wake up the body.

The gym opened up at some ungodly hour in the morning and stayed relatively busy through the rest of the day. Bonnie smiled hello to me from behind the reception desk as I scanned my membership card. The gym was busy, filled with the professional sect, stopping by after getting out of work and before going home. I changed in the locker room and set to work on my triceps, alternating between dips and various exercises with the free weights. I wasn't in the mood to watch the girls on the treadmill, so I finished my workout relatively quickly. I did four different exercises for my abs, showered up, and I was done.

By the time I walked out to my car it was dark and cool outside. I always felt better after going to the gym, but I still had no idea where I was going with the Jessica Stanchion case. Truth be told, the only thing I had to hand Michael Stanchion so far was the bill for my sandwich.

I drove home, parked the car, and walked up the stairs and into my house. I didn't have any messages on my machine, and the television service was shut off as I hadn't paid my cable bill since I bought the place. I turned on the radio, poured myself a glass of orange juice, and cooked up some pasta.

In an effort to atone for sleeping through a majority of my high school history classes, I had bought a copy of Woodward and Bernstein's *All the President's Men*. I was tired of not being able to laugh at Nixon jokes at parties. After I ate my dinner I read for the better part of two hours and then, simply for the lack of anything better to do, went to bed.

12

Last December

It was like a fairy tale. She was the princess, and Tommy was Prince Charming who rode in on his white horse and swept her off her feet.

And Jessica could not stop smiling.

They'd only been dating for a little over a month, but it seemed like forever.

Jessica had never had a boyfriend before. She had attended private all-girl schools, and curfews and her parents' rules had kept her in studying during her free time on nights and weekends. She didn't mind. She saw the logic in her father's requests. He was right, of course; all the hard work would pay off in the future, and like he always reminded her, "her future started now."

But Tommy wasn't a distraction from her work. If anything, she actually worked even harder now. She had to account for all her lessons and projects before she could use the phone, and even then she was only allowed to talk for a limited time. But that was OK too, because Tommy was busy with practice, or his job, or his own schoolwork, and couldn't talk on the phone for hours like some of the other girls said they did.

She worked extra hard to prove to Daddy that this wasn't a mistake either. If her grades slipped, even a little, she knew he would put her back in Queens Academy. But she also worked harder because she wanted Tommy to be proud of her. That was an extra incentive that made her study even more. One time at lunch, Marcia, the girl with the pretty dark hair, said she was failing her algebra class and just couldn't understand any of it. Tommy spoke up and said, "Hey Jess, you're good in math. Could you give Marcia a hand?"

She liked it when he called her Jess. Her parents and all their friends and her teachers always referred to her as "Jessica." He always called her Jess and looked straight at her and smiled when he said it.

She helped Marcia with her homework, and Marcia was so appreciative and Jessica was so happy because Tommy had asked her to help one of his friends and she hadn't let him down.

She liked making Tommy happy. She liked it when he smiled just at her. She liked the butterflies she got in her stomach when she knew she was going to see him. She liked the way she could wrap his varsity jacket around her and it would keep her warm. She liked the way the other boys and girls at school referred to them as "Jess 'n' Tommy."

The first time he kissed her they were sitting in the dugout on the playing fields. It was raining and all after-school practices had been cancelled. They were sitting on the visiting team's bench watching the rain. It was cold, and Tommy pulled her close to keep her warm, and then he leaned in and kissed her. She thought fireworks were going to erupt all around her.

Mother convinced Daddy that it was OK for her to go to the Winter Dance and even took her shopping to get a new dress. She was very nervous—this was her first dance—but once she got there everything was perfect. Tommy looked so handsome, and took her dancing, and pulled out her chair for her at their table, a table that was filled with so many pretty girls and their dates. Everybody was so nice. Marcia even came over and sat next to her during dinner and told her how much she liked her earrings.

Of course, she had to leave early. That was Daddy's compromise. Her mother called ten minutes after Jessica got home. Jessica started to tell her mother everything that happened at the dance but her mother had to go help Daddy greet some important people who would help him run for office. She was just calling to make sure Jessica got home.

Jessica understood. Her parents were very busy. They had many important things to do. She went upstairs and hung up her dress carefully. She changed into her pajamas and put the rose that Tommy had given her in water and placed it on her dresser. She smiled to herself as she looked at it. Nobody had ever given her flowers before.

Then she sat down at her desk and dutifully opened up one of her textbooks.

It's funny, the things that jog your memory. I grew up in St. Luke's Orphanage in Boston, Massachusetts. It was a brick building that housed about twenty kids. There was a decent playground in the back and an overgrown baseball diamond three blocks to the east. As kids, we didn't know anything else; this was our home. And, as kids, we simply made the best of our situation.

The orphanage was run by three nuns: Sister Margaret, Sister Sarah, and Sister Katherine, and they attended to our daily needs, giving us chores and giving us our schooling. My primary years in education consisted mainly of getting whacked on a daily basis with a yardstick. Shocking, I know.

Sisters Margaret and Sarah were responsible for doling out the punishments during the day; Sister Katherine always had the night shift. Whenever I would sneak downstairs in the middle of the night I would find Katherine sitting in the parlor reading, listening to the radio, or knitting a blanket that I never saw finished.

We had a strict curfew and weren't supposed to be out of bed after ten, but she never chastised me. She would always invite me in to sit with her. We would talk, she'd read to me, and we'd listen to the radio. She would educate me about music, introducing me to Ray Charles, Aretha Franklin, and the Rolling Stones, a group she called her "guilty pleasure." Sometimes we would walk outside in the early, early morning, pick up the newspaper right off the delivery truck, and walk the three blocks to the baseball diamond to watch the sunrise.

Katherine would say many times in conversation, "Everything happens exactly as it should, Samuel." I didn't particularly care for this comment. I didn't get much pleasure in thinking I was supposed to end up at an orphanage, that I was supposed to be abandoned by my parents. As I grew up, I put my own slant on the meaning behind Sister Katherine's words. She was talking about trust in a higher power. I came to believe that things happen as they should because previous actions have put them into place. Find out those previous actions, and you'll find out the reasons for the way things are now. Digging through the past can explain the present; puzzle pieces put together to give the complete picture. The secretary at the high school had reminded me of Sister Katherine. She was warm and welcoming and had a sense of inner peace about her. I liked her. And it was because of her that I awoke the next morning with Katherine's words ringing in my head.

I needed a fuller picture of Jessica Stanchion's world to find out what had led to her final fate. That meant digging into her family. The Internet would only get me so far, and it would be generic coverage at best. More substantial resources were needed to delve into the Stanchion's activities in the local community. Fortunately, I had two: the campus library in the next town over and the living breathing resource known as Everett Jones.

It was seven in the morning, and I knew Everett had already been up for at least an hour, but I decided to be courteous and leave a message on his office voice mail asking him to look into the background of the Stanchion family, particularly Michael and his son. It was just a hunch, but I didn't see Mrs. Stanchion as having any type of questionable background. If there was any dirt on the other two, Everett would have it for me within twenty-four hours. Ten to one if I spoke with him instead of his machine, he'd be able to recite half of it from memory already.

Sadly, the only thing left for me was the prospect of tackling the library alone. Not exactly my first choice, but what the hell. Duty was calling. I grabbed a quick shower, got dressed, and headed over to campus.

Chuck Berry was finishing up "Roll over Beethoven" when I arrived on campus. I stopped at the Dunkin' Donuts at the top of the hill and bought a bagel and cream cheese. That would have to serve as breakfast. I finally found a parking spot at the base of the hill and walked up to the library. The last time I was here, it was during the summer session, and the campus was empty. Now, halfway into the first semester, the campus and probably the library as well would be packed with students. The only thing I had going for me was the fact that no way in hell would any self-respecting college student be awake at eight thirty in the morning.

I reached the library and walked up the stone steps, through the glass doors, and into the foyer. The campus library was everything you expected a library to be: immaculate, proud, and way too damn quiet. Even with the relatively early hour, students were already milling about. I walked through the turnstile, past the help desk, and down the stairs to the basement of the library, which housed the main artery of available research equipment. A room at the far end of the floor contained computers tied into the campus library archives, and not only could they divulge every iota of available information available to you, they also had idiot-proof instructions hanging on the wall in front of them detailing how to use them. This was higher education.

I sat at a computer situated in the back row, right behind a young lady dressed all in black with a pasty white complexion that was even more enhanced by her deep rouge lipstick. It's a good thing we were in the basement. If sunlight hit her, she'd probably melt.

I typed in Jessica Stanchion's name. One article surfaced where she was simply mentioned as the daughter of Michael Stanchion, who was currently running for governor. The only other statements were the numerous articles that had run in the Providence Journal detailing the discovery of her dead body.

I thought it was a sad commentary that the only time you made the paper was when you were dead at seventeen, but the only time Vanessa Stanchion's name was mentioned was when she was referred to as "the doting wife of Michael." That might have been sadder.

Stanchion's son was in the papers once, in an article detailing his prison sentence for dealing heroin. But that wasn't news. Stanchion had alluded to that at our first meeting. Michael Stanchion himself won the grand prize, as I found a total of 29 articles dealing with him. Most of them were trivial; community work, editorials, and committees on which he had served. Sifting through them all, I was only able to find three articles that held the promise of resembling anything relevant. Two of them were recent and dealt with his bid for the election, one giving an overview of his life accomplishments, the second a declaration of his campaign initiatives. The third article was two years old and apparently was Stanchion's claim to fame in lawyer-world. According to the article, he had represented alleged mobster Corey Runter, who had been brought up on charges by one Matthew Townhouse. Stanchion lost the case, but apparently his defense of Runter was considered remarkable, as he was able to convince the court to dismiss over half the evidence the prosecution brought into court. The case was referenced in one of the other articles as "what put Michael Stanchion on the map and kept him there."

I'd spent almost an hour in the library, which, incidentally, ranked as my second-longest stay in a building of this nature, and had come up with next to nothing in terms of pertinent information. I was one step away from asking Stanchion if he had any scrapbooks lying around that I could borrow in hopes of finding a clue. I wrote the names Corey Runter and Matthew Townhouse down on a piece of scrap paper and put it in my pocket. I got up, winked at the vampire in front of me, made the sign of the cross, and left.

There was a message on my phone when I returned to my car. As I had aged considerably since the last time anyone called me, I had to ask one of the college students walking by for help in remembering how to retrieve my messages. Once properly dialed, I heard Gloria Hurdtz's voice streaming from my voicemail. She was breathing heavily and told me she couldn't stop thinking about me since we met yesterday. She had to see me, and she'd be lounging in a bubble bath at seven that evening with a bottle of champagne. The door would be unlocked.

Actually that didn't happen at all. Gloria's voice was indeed on my voicemail, but she had her breathing quite under control and told me in a curt manner that she had some information that could be helpful in the case and asked if I would be so inclined to meet her at the Red Stone at three. Apparently she would be able to restrain herself until we met.

The Red Stone was a small upscale café that carried sixty-three specialized martinis and one draft beer. Chances are the management wouldn't let me park on their street let alone enter their establishment, but I wasn't about to get into an argument with Gloria over bar choices. She said she had information, which meant she already had more clues than I did.

I dialed the high school. The phone was answered on the third ring, and once again I was talking with Doreen the secretary, my elderly lover. I asked her to leave a message for Gloria stating that three was fine, and she gave me a response that fell somewhere between disapproval and irritation. I got the feeling that Doreen fielded many calls for Gloria of this nature.

I drove home. At this point my best options were to eat an early lunch and wait for the hand of God to reach down and point me in the right direction. I pulled into my driveway, climbed the stairs to my deck, and walked in through my kitchen door.

Inside, seated at my kitchen table and waiting patiently for me, was a very large, very well-dressed man. He wore an impeccable black pin-striped suit with freshly polished matching black wingtips. His dark hair was newly cut and slicked back and he smelled of expensive cologne. His eyes were a clouded-over grey that seemed focused on nothing in particular, and when he spoke his voice came from a faraway place.

"Good morning." He greeted me with no apparent concern. He looked at me as if I was a guest in his presence.

"Good morning." I leaned back against the countertop.

"We need to have a discussion."

"Business or pleasure?"

"Business."

The chairs at my kitchen table are not that large. This man was. He did not look that comfortable.

"Why don't we pretend we're two civilized people and conduct business in my office," I said, gesturing in that direction.

He heaved himself up with a bit of effort and walked casually down the hallway. My office was the second room on the left. I followed him in. He took a seat in one of my client chairs and I sat behind my desk. I almost felt professional.

The gentleman took his time looking around and then, seeming satisfied, crossed his legs and clasped his hands together.

"You are Samuel Miller?"

"Wouldn't you be embarrassed if you broke into the wrong house."

He stopped talking for a moment and looked at me for the first time.

"A simple yes or no will do."

"Yes, I am Samuel Miller."

"You have been hired by Michael Stanchion?"

"Yes again."

"Not any longer."

"Pardon me?" I asked, cocking my head to the side the way I'd seen Bruce Willis do in a movie once.

He continued as if I hadn't even spoken.

"As of now you are no longer working for Michael Stanchion. You will no longer investigate the death of Jessica Stanchion. And you are no longer looking into the past of the Stanchion family. You will be paid an extra five thousand dollars for your trouble, and you will immediately start to seek employment elsewhere."

"You mentioned that this was a discussion. Do I get to speak any time soon?"

"Paying you for your time is one way to ensure your cooperation," he went on. "But there are, of course, other ways."

A gun flashed into his hand. It hadn't been there a minute ago. He didn't aim it at me; he just held it out and studied it thoughtfully. Of course I had a gun too. It was locked in my top desk drawer. I pictured myself lying on my deathbed explaining to Lil that I got shot because I couldn't pull my keys out fast enough. She'd be so disgusted she probably wouldn't even come to my funeral.

The man stood up. The gun was still in his hand.

"I trust we have reached a mutual consensus."

He turned and walked out of the room as if he didn't have a care in the world. I heard the door slam as he left. A host of thoughts were running through my mind, the most prominent being I needed better locks. I walked to the window and watched the man cross the street to the vacant beach parking lot. He got into a black four-door Lincoln Continental and drove off down the street. It looked remarkably like the Lincoln I saw at Stanchion's yesterday.

Probably more than one Lincoln Continental in Rhode Island.

Probably no such thing as coincidence either.

I had asked for the hand of God to help me, and instead I had gotten His middle finger. I knew where I ranked. Being asked, and not in a very polite manner I might add, to simply walk away from Stanchion's case looked remarkably like a clue. Especially since I was fired by someone other than Michael Stanchion himself. I took out the piece of paper from the library and looked at the names. Matthew Townhouse and Corey Runter. Runter was a gangster, and I had no idea what Townhouse's deal was, but the two of them were the closest lead I had in terms of associates of Stanchion.

I needed someone smarter than me. Usually that meant I could have a conversation with the carpet and come out in second place. I decided to reach for the brass ring instead and placed a call to Everett to compare notes. Everett's secretary was ever-efficient, as only Everett's secretary would be, and answered the phone midway through the first ring.

"Security Outfitters," she said in a voice that bit through the phone lines with a crispness found only in good starch and excellent scotch, though I wouldn't advise mixing the two.

"Everett Jones, please."

"Certainly. May I ask who's calling please?"

"Pope Pius III."

"Certainly. One moment please."

She put me on hold. Based upon my initial interaction, Security Outfitters' first line of defense might need a little upgrade.

A few words about Everett. He is, without a doubt, one of the smartest people I know. Granted, compared with the rest of the clientele with which I associate, Lil notwithstanding, that doesn't say much. But here's a guy retired from the Secret Service, one of the most dedicated and hard-working persons to ever come from that detail by the way, who has more than earned a good stay of relaxation for the rest of his days. But instead of retiring, he stays on as a senior advisor, working as a liaison with the FBI. Now, he doesn't have to do any of this, mind you, because he has already shrewdly invested his money in the stock market, making himself, by my standards anyway, incredibly fucking rich.

He met me during my extremely brief stint with the U.S. Marshals, and for reasons beyond my comprehension, pursued an active friendship with me. He finally stepped down after years of service with the government and opened a tavern in Philadelphia with Lil, his wife Nicole, and me. Now, after selling our restaurant, he's started up his own aforementioned security consulting network, which, like anything he touches, has become immensely successful. He has a wonderful wife in Nicole, possesses a wealth of informational resources, governmental or otherwise, and for reasons known only to him, will often sit upon my right shoulder, a six-foot-four Jiminy Cricket, and prevail upon me as my own personal conscience. In short, he is simply a truly gifted and phenomenal person. I'm usually ready to punch him after our second conversation of the day.

"Samuel." His voice interrupted the silence on the line.

"Shouldn't you be addressing me as 'Your Holiness'?"

"Caller ID, Sam. First line in security defense."

I stand corrected.

Everett didn't wait for me to ask a question, he simply started right in addressing what I'd asked this morning.

"I've gathered some poignant information that could prove quite illuminating and advantageous as you continue facilitating a working relationship with your current employer."

When I first met Everett, I carried around a pocket dictionary just so I could maintain my part of the conversation. After three weeks I just stopped talking.

"What do you have?"

"Some details that prove interesting. Michael Stanchion is married to the former Vanessa Tiles. They have two children, a son Aaron who is currently serving a prison sentence, and a daughter Jessica, recently deceased."

He spoke into the phone as if he was reading facts from a history book.

"Your employer is a high-profile attorney who divides his time between cases in Rhode Island and Massachusetts and is currently running for governor of Rhode Island. Of his more famous cases, the one that bears scrutiny is his defense of alleged mobster Corey Runter."

"The one back in the Townhouse trial?"

"The very same."

Finally I contributed something to the conversation. I did this mainly so I wouldn't feel like I had to give half my paycheck to Everett at the end of the phone call. He of course went on to expound in detail upon the mere surface material I had collected at the library. And yes, I did keep in mind the fact that I had been working on this case for a day and a half and he only a scant six hours.

Mattie Townhouse, according to Everett's reports, became famous when he turned state's witness and pointed the finger at computer-industrialist Frederick Giles. Giles had become one of the most powerful individuals in the software industry, but only because Townhouse had leaked him fragments of programs from the giant computer corporation Visitron. Giles would then infiltrate the programs he was given and create computer viruses that were designed to go off in six-month's time. When the computers that had installed the mass-marketed Visitron software started experiencing viruses, Giles rode in on his white horse with prepackaged software guaranteed to cure the viruses and then sold his version of the Visitron software, complete with improvements and upgrades.

It worked for four years, making Giles a very rich man and one of the heads of industry in New England. Townhouse got cold feet and went to the feds when he learned that Giles was also working with Corey Runter, the sole proprietor of the prostitution rings in southern Massachusetts. Runter would take the profits from his girls and invest them in Giles' stock right before he released his next product. In return, Giles received cash up front to mass market his products.

To make a long story short, the three of them got to go to trial. Stanchion, according to Everett, stepped in and convinced everyone to look at Runter as a victim of insider trading. His alleged involvement in prostitution was never discussed, and as a result he received the same sentence as Giles, two years at a minimum security prison in Baltimore, the equivalent of a convict's country club. Townhouse was placed in the witness protection program for the rest of his life, and both Giles and Runter were out in six months because of good behavior. Martha Stewart would be proud.

"Loud rumors have been circulating that as payback for his intervention in the trial, Corey Runter has been lending a helping hand to Stanchion's bid for office. He's in charge of prostitution, but as an arm of the organized crime circuit. If he's lending a helping hand, then in turn, the mob is lending a helping hand. Which means—"

"The mob might not like somebody poking around and stirring things up. Understood. I think I've just been on the receiving end of that same helping hand. But if he's in with the mob, why even come to me? Why not just ask his buddy Runter for help?"

"I'm sure he did. But there's a big difference between paying off a debt and meddling in a family's affairs. Stanchion might not be in deep enough to warrant that kind of help. Or he might not want to be in that deep. What happened with you?"

"Had a conversation with a well-dressed gorilla who suggested it would be in my best interests to walk away from the case."

"And?"

"Never really done what's in my best interests."

"Be careful."

Fifteen seconds of static air passed while we adjusted ourselves from business to personal.

"How's Nicole?" I asked.

"Wonderful," Everett answered. "Promoted again. At the start of January she'll be working with the FBI full-time."

"Congratulations to her," I said.

"I'll tell her," Everett said with a hint of resignation in his voice. Everett was a traditionalist enough to want Nicole to be a stay-at-home wife, smart enough to realize that was a role that would never work for her, and a decent enough person to feel guilty about wanting this in the first place. It was a continuous cycle with him. "How's Lil?"

"Having bumper stickers printed up as we speak that read 'Buy a house from me or I'll shoot you.'"

Everett chuckled. "Some things change…"

"And some things shouldn't," I finished. "Thanks for the heads up."

"Stay in touch."

"Absolutely."

We hung up. I sat in my office mulling over what Everett had told me. If it was true, and I'd yet to have an experience where Everett was wrong, then it put Jessica's murder in a whole new light. Was she killed in a mob-related incident? A warning of some kind to Michael Stanchion? I still wanted it to be Tommy Bates, more out of a desire to have an excuse to shoot him than anything else. Leave it to Everett to answer my questions by simultaneously sliding more questions in. My head hurt.

I had a little time to waste before my lunch date. I unlocked my drawer and took out my gun—probably wouldn't need to shoot Gloria Hurdtz, but I'd feel even stupider if she killed me over a martini. No reason to waste a drink. I locked my doors, although now I was questioning why I even bothered, and drove over to the police station.

I was always amazed that a police station was the place where you brought criminals—bank robbers, arsonists, rapists—and yet you never saw so much as a scuffle outside the headquarters. This time was no different. I drove up and parked, and the station was once again a model of tranquility. I walked through the doors and over to the receptionist. She was a large, well-rounded woman named Sadie. She had brown hair that fell past her shoulders and wore a pink sweater with a yellow scarf tied around her neck. She greeted me with an ear-to-ear smile as I approached.

"Mr. Miller. It's been a while."

"That's only because normally I'm being hauled past you in cuffs, and nobody will let me say hello."

She giggled and I leaned over the desk and gave her a kiss on the cheek.

"Just on the cheek?" she asked feigning dejection.

"Sadie, you are wearing neon-power-pink lipstick, sweetheart. If I get anywhere near that, I'll be waving planes into the airport every time I show my left profile."

She giggled again.

"What can I do for you?"

"I need to look through your mug shots. Think I could do that?"

"Sure, no problem. I'll have Carl hook you up with a computer."

It used to be that you had to pore through endless photo albums full of notorious felons until you recognized a face. Now that we were in the digital age, you got to pore though endless pictures of notorious felons on a computer screen until you recognized a face. Modern technology.

Sadie made a quick phone call, and within five minutes an officer opened the door to the inner sanctum of the police department and took me over to a computer terminal. If you shut your eyes, you'd think you were in an office or a newsroom. All you heard was the continuous tapping on computer keyboards and the telephones ringing nonstop. All a pleasant mirage for those uninitiated into the actual world of a police officer.

"You looking for anyone in particular?" Carl asked as he booted up the program.

"Corey Runter."

He laughed. "You go straight to the top, don't you?"

"Apparently," I said.

"Here you go." Carl got up and gave me his seat. "Not a huge record on him. That's how you know you've made it to the big leagues. The true criminals manage to stay off the charts."

I thanked him and sat down. Corey Runter had been convicted three times since 1981, according to the information in front of me, with thirteen months being his longest stay. Looking at his pictures, one might say he aged nicely, and one would also say he was most definitely not the man who had been in my kitchen late this morning. I was feeling less appreciated with each passing minute.

Corey Runter was a slim man with a narrow face and short blond hair. He had what looked to be an artificially tanned face, but who could tell from a computer screen, and a large nose and prominent forehead. Basically he looked like he could be an executive at any one of a dozen corporations. If one called prostitution a corporation, well then, he fit right in.

There were a few "known associates" pictured at the bottom of the page, but none who resembled my noontime visitor. I was gathering so much useless information I could start compiling the "Lowlifes" version of Trivial Pursuit.

I logged off the computer and walked back through the office to the reception area.

"Leaving already?" Sadie asked.

I nodded. I asked if I could borrow a piece of paper and an envelope. Sadie handed them over, and using the pen attached by a chain to the desk, I scribbled out a quick note to Lucille. I put it in the envelope and wrote her name on it.

"Would you put that in Lieutenant Simon's mail, Sadie?" I asked.

"Of course, Sam," she smiled. "Come back again soon."

"Be careful what you wish for," I grinned, and walked out the building.

Last December

Politics agreed with Michael Stanchion.

Put on a suit, put on a smile, and shake hands with everyone near you. Then just step back and watch things happen. And things were happening quite rapidly. Sometimes he was introduced as the next candidate for governor, other times people were introduced to him. Sometimes the fundraisers were held for him, other times he attended fundraisers for other politicos. Meet and greet, forge rapports, build a network. This really was easy.

He was starting to create an image in the community. And when it all came down to it, politics was all about image. How you were perceived, where you were seen, and who you were seen with. Politics was covered by the media, and if people liked what they saw, they liked you. Surround yourself with the right people, and acceptance was automatic.

Corey Runter had been very generous with his help. He'd used his girls as bargaining chips to basically insure that the right people jumped on Stanchion's platform. It quickly became an expected occurrence that a small group of very attractive women accompany Stanchion wherever he went. This in turn guaranteed a solid turnout at Stanchion's gatherings, and one or two hours with Runter's girls translated to confident assurances that certain prominent individuals would indeed be backing Michael Stanchion.

Stanchion himself was encouraged to partake in the pleasures being offered. Sort of a finishing touch on the "you scratched my back; now I'll scratch yours" mentality of Corey Runter. Sample the goods. Get a piece. Live it up. You've been working hard. You're going to be working harder. Take a minute and smell those roses.

Michael didn't look at it as cheating on Vanessa, really. This was a gift. That's all. A door prize. Only instead of getting tickets to the Celtics or a flat screen TV, he was getting an hour with Blond Number Four. He didn't even view them as actual human beings. They were simply cogs in the machinery of the electoral process. Shake some hands, get a drink, have some sex. All part of the process.

It was a good process.

And it would almost certainly get even better.

The Red Stone was tucked away on a little side street a half mile away from the beach. It offered valet parking even though the parking lot only held eight cars and most people parked on the street, but that aspect alone spoke volumes about its rank in the restaurant businesses in town. A mini water fountain constructed of rock adorned the front patio and sent a continuous waterfall down over the stone and flowers that decorated the lawn. A giant red stone sat at the very top of the fountain, giving the restaurant both a landmark and name. The fountain was big enough to be pretty, but not so big as to be in the way, and no one ever saw a drunk taking a piss in the fountain itself. Things such as that simply did not happen at the Red Stone.

I parked on the street and walked up the steps to the main entrance. A light rain had started when I left the police station and had built up to small and steady on my ride over. A rainy afternoon in October. A perfect afternoon to spend in a bar. Although as I thought about it I was hard pressed to find a bad one.

The bar itself was a marble horseshoe and, as it was quarter to three in the afternoon, was quite empty. The staff milled around dressed in white tuxedo shirts and bow ties, looking like they were trying not to look like they were uncomfortable. I sat down at the bar, and a bartender with hazel eyes and midnight-black hair pulled back in a ponytail appeared before me. I ordered a Jameson's on the rocks, it materialized seemingly magically in front of me, and the bartender was gone. The Cheshire Cat stayed around longer. Left more of an impression too.

There was a small TV in the corner on the far wall running MSNBC headlines, but the sound was off, and it was too far away to see. After a closer inspection of the bar area, there didn't seem to be any place one could sit and actually see the TV. Maybe people didn't come to the Red Stone to watch TV. Soft violin music was piped in through unseen speakers, and as I looked around the restaurant, I counted four other patrons in the entire building. One couple was seated side by side at a table by the giant picture window, nuzzling and whispering to each other over a bottle of wine. The other two were seated by the door and seemed to be going over legal documents while sipping multicolored martinis.

I turned my attention back to my nonexistent bartender and the TV I couldn't see and sipped my drink. Before I was a third of the way through, Gloria Hurdtz walked through the front door. She stopped and took a brief look around, caught my eye, waved, smiled, and came over. She wore a purple windbreaker to brave the rain, but had ignored the hood, and her hair was a little damp. She had worn it down today, and it fell to the top of her shoulders. Her blouse was white and made of silk and bordered on see-through. If she hadn't worn the windbreaker it would have been. Her skirt was simple and short, and a deep blue, as were her heels. She smiled at me again when she reached the bar, draped her jacket over her chair, and sat down.

"Thanks for meeting me," she said.

"Thanks for the invitation."

A male bartender appeared this time. He had wide shoulders and dark hair cut short. He put a green tinted martini down in front of Gloria even though she hadn't placed an order. He didn't even look at me.

"Your principal require you to dress that extravagantly at school?"

"I went home and changed." She gave me a sideways glance. "You only stared at my legs the last time."

"Fair enough."

She crossed her legs and sipped her drink. I waited in silence while she did. Some things deserve to be enjoyed in a certain sequence.

When she placed her glass back on the bar top I asked, "So what do you know about Tommy Bates?"

"Tommy Bates? Well, my day was fine, thank you for asking. And, no, I didn't have any trouble getting over here in the rain either, thank you for asking again."

I could feel a smile tugging at the corners of my mouth.

"Aren't you at least going to tell me how nice I look?" she said, turning to look at me.

"Stunning."

"That's better," she laughed. She took another sip of her drink, this one a bit larger than her first. "So what's it like being a private detective?"

"Same as your job, only I get to shoot whoever annoys me."

She giggled and took a third swallow of her drink. Hers was almost gone. Mine was still two-thirds full.

"Are they all as handsome as you?"

"More so. That's why I moved to Rhode Island. Less competition."

"Where are you from?"

"Philly, by way of Boston."

She finished her drink. The bartender had another one on the bar before her glass touched the counter.

"And you came here? Why?"

"Ambience."

She smiled. She picked up her drink and swiveled in her chair so her knees touched my leg.

"And now you're investigating the death of Jessica Stanchion. How'd you get that job?"

"Her father hired me."

"And you think Tommy did it?"

"I don't know. Do you?"

She shook her head.

"Tommy's a good soul. He's handsome and funny and smart. He's every girl's dream. I'd have an easier time believing Jessica killed someone to keep Tommy to herself."

"That's surprising. Everyone else I've spoken with says Jessica was one of the sweetest people they knew."

She took a drink from her glass and shrugged her shoulders.

"I'm just saying, you know, Tommy had no reason to kill her."

She set her drink back down. It was half empty. My glass, on the other hand, had become full again as all the ice had melted.

"I'd be careful though, Tommy's dad might not like you harassing his son."

"When did I harass him?"

"I don't know that you did," she said quickly. "I'm just trying to give you a heads-up. Help out."

"Thanks."

We were quiet for a bit, listening to the rain and watching it through the windows. Gloria returned her attention to me and leaned back in her chair and studied me for a moment. She rested her elbow on the bar and leaned her head against her hand. She smiled.

"So."

"So," I replied, looking back at her. I took my money out of my pocket, counted out some bills, and placed them on the bar. I stood up. "Thanks for your help, Ms. Hurdtz. If you think of anything else that might be relevant to the case, please give me a call."

She lifted her head off her hand. "You're leaving?" She sounded almost incredulous. She settled back into her chair and smiled to herself. "Hmf. Two drinks in and I usually have to help whoever I'm with get my clothes off."

I smiled as graciously as I could. "Some other time. May I walk you to your car?"

"No," she said. A fresh drink had appeared in front of her. "I'll stay here. Someone else will come along."

Someone else always does.

I was awoken at three in the morning by my ringing phone. Two phone calls in two days. This was a record. I fumbled for the receiver and put it to my ear.

"Yeah."

"You want me to ask Stanchion if we can exhume his daughter's body?!" Lucille's voice barked through the phone wires. "Are you out of your mind?"

"Good morning Lucille," I said. She didn't return any greeting, so I continued. "I latched onto this kid Tom Bates at her school. I thought maybe he killed her because he got her pregnant."

"You have got to be shitting me."

I waited while she collected herself. When she spoke again it was with deliberate control.

"Sam, I am going to say this again. We are a professional police force. We do this for a living. When a teenage girl dies unnaturally, the top reasons why almost always involve sex. Of course we had her checked out. She was not pregnant; in fact, she was still a virgin. And yes, we pulled Tom Bates in for questioning too."

"I don't like him."

"I don't like him either. But if I convicted people solely on personal opinion, you would be serving thirteen consecutive life sentences."

"Now you're just being mean."

"Here's something else you're not going to like, Sam. We've been asked by Bates' father to file a restraining order against you. As of now you are to cease and desist any and all association with young Tommy Bates."

"You're just full of good news, aren't you?"

"Have a good night, Sam."

I hung up the phone and lay back in bed staring at the ceiling. In the past twenty-four hours I had been kicked off my case, refused sex with an open and sexually ambitious young woman, and been told by the police to stay away from the only concrete suspect I had.

It's a wonder I was able to get back to sleep at all.

I woke up around seven thirty, went to the gym for a little over an hour, and took a long hot shower. I drove out of the parking lot at nine twenty-five feeling fresh and unemployed. I headed north up Route 1 towards East Greenwich. Lucille had said Stanchion spent the mornings in his office before heading out on the campaign trail in the afternoon. If he was a creature of habit, all signs pointed to him being in his office after ten. Today I would be too.

I took the exit for East Greenwich and careened down the hill of hills to Main Street. Down two blocks to my left stood the former Search for Salvation headquarters, which had been bought out and turned into a glassware store that specialized in selling bongs of all shapes and sizes. I'm not sure too many people noticed the difference.

I turned right and made a quick left into the parking lot of Michael Stanchion's office. It was hard to miss. A giant placard with his face plastered on it had been erected right in front of the building. The billboard showed him smiling a big toothy grin, but I'm sure he was crying on the inside. I walked into his building and was greeted by a woman with short curly hair wearing glasses.

"Is his royal highness in?" I asked, and walked towards the only closed door behind her.

"Excuse me, but you can't just—"

"Morning, Mike," I said pushing the door open and stepping inside.

"Mr. Stanchion, I don't know who—"

I slammed the door in her face.

Michael Stanchion sat behind a very large and very fake-but-made-to-look-like-it-was-real oak desk. He had been examining the contents of a manila folder, and if he was startled when I walked in, he did an excellent job of keeping his composure. He was dressed in a dark suit with a blue shirt and a yellow tie, which I'm sure he considered powerful-looking, but truth be told, his power was more in his persona than in his clothes. The phone on his desk rang. He picked it up and after a moment spoke into it, saying, "No, Nancy, everything's all right. Thank you." His secretary was persistent, I'll give her that. I took a seat in front of his desk while he hung up the phone.

"Mr. Miller," he said, looking me straight in the eye. "This is a surprise." He paused and we sat in a prolonged and awkward silence. He finally followed up with, "What can I do for you?"

"Usually, Mike, when I've been hired by somebody, that's my line."

"I see." He frowned and looked thoughtful for a minute. "Are you coming to me with some news?"

"Actually Mike, the biggest news I have is that apparently I've been fired."

He tapped his thumbs against his lips four times before replying.

"Yes, yes…I see. I hope you don't take that personally. It has nothing to do with your credentials or anything. It's just that, well, with the election next month and all, well, covert investigations and such, it's just not the proper time for any of that."

"Is that your decision or Corey Runter's?"

He stopped moving so suddenly I wanted to check to see if he was breathing.

"I'm afraid I'm going to have to ask you to leave, Mr. Miller," he said in a quiet voice.

"Mike, two days ago you came to me desperate to find your daughter's killer. I start poking around, and the next thing I know I have King Kong junior waiting for me in my house telling me that either dead or five Gs richer, I'm getting off the case. You want to be straight with me and tell me what the hell's going on, please?"

Stanchion was sitting in front of a picture window that let in an enormous amount of sunlight. We only had to hear the glass shatter once to realize shots were being fired at us through it. I yelled at Stanchion to get down, but we were both on the floor before the words were out of my mouth. We heard three more bullets hit the wall and then silence. I drew my gun and ran out the door, telling Stanchion to stay down. I yelled at the secretary to stay where she was and was actually half surprised she hadn't buzzed into the office to check on his welfare when she heard the shots.

I ran around the side of the building in the direction from where the shots were fired, but no one was there. I turned back towards the building just in time to see Stanchion and his secretary get into their respective cars and moments later drive off, leaving me standing in front of the billboard with his smiling face.

"Really, Mike, I'm OK. Thanks for asking," I said out loud.

I sounded like Gloria Hurdtz.

Jerk.

The shooter had left. The shootees had left. I was the only one stupid enough to still be standing on the front lawn. The hell with it. I decided to pack it up and go home too.

I took the scenic route and stopped off in North Kingstown for lunch. I ordered a club sandwich and picked a piece of glass out of my hair. I thought about putting it in my sandwich and then complaining to the management so I could get a free meal, but that would probably end up being the first of many successive steps towards a life of crime that would then culminate in me cutting off a finger and hiding it in a bowl of chili. I decided against it and breathed a sigh of relief as I realized the years of embarrassment and imprisonment I had just narrowly escaped.

I took my time driving, and it was mid-afternoon by the time I finally got home. Lil's jeep was parked in the driveway. The mood I was in, if anyone other then her or Kermit the Frog was waiting for me inside, I'd just put a bullet in their head and grab a drink. Hell, I'd shoot Kermit too and sell his legs to the delicatessen down the street.

When I walked inside I found Lil lounging in my living room looking over some paperwork. Her hair was up in a bun, with a few stray hairs falling down and framing her face. She was wearing a red blouse and a tan skirt. She stood up to greet me and gave me a smile that could jump start the space shuttle.

"Fuck me, are you a welcome sight," I said as she came over and kissed me hello.

"You always know just the right thing to say."

We walked back into the living room and sat down on the couch.

"To what do I owe the pleasure of your company?" I asked.

"Haven't seen you in a couple days, babe. This is as close as I get to missing you."

"You're just horny."

"That too."

I recounted the exploits of my last two days, including my noble declining of Ms. Hurdtz's advances. Lil listened to me with the same interest she gives all my stories, which is to say much more than they deserve. When I finished, she pulled me up with both hands.

"What you need," she said, unbuttoning my shirt, "is a good, long bath. And if you're good, I'll wash your back."

She pulled off my shirt and pushed me in the direction of the hallway.

"If you're really good," she called from the living room, "I'll do your front."

I walked into the bathroom and finished getting undressed.

"If you're really, really good, I'll do your—"

I couldn't hear her finish over the running water.

Thank God she followed me in.

—21—

Later in the evening we holed up in the living room and ordered some Chinese food. Lil was barefoot and wearing blue jeans and one of my old flannel shirts, which looked indescribably better on her than it ever had on me.

"I never realized how good that shirt looks."

"That's because you don't wear it with the right attitude."

She used her chopsticks to gracefully carry a piece of sweet and sour chicken to her mouth. No sauce was spilled anywhere, and she held the chicken effortlessly in the air while she nibbled off a bite. I had trouble opening the fortune cookie.

"I spent my day at the State House."

"Doing what?" I asked.

"Soliciting."

"Going back to your old tricks?"

"Hardly. But if you want to sell the big houses, you have to go where the money is. It's all about clientele, sweetie."

"Isn't soliciting illegal, especially on government property?"

"It is," she said, biting into an egg roll, "but I smiled and wore this skirt, which does a great job showing off my ass, so..."

"So people came up to you."

"I never left the front steps."

"You are going back to your old tricks."

"Darling, I never left them. I simply switched vocations. But I think I found something that might help you."

"How?"

Lil passed me the rest of the chicken and broccoli and opened the wonton soup.

"One of the gentlemen who greeted me works on Stanchion's campaign. He was stopping by to drop off some forms and ended up inviting me to a fundraiser the day after tomorrow. A lot of bigwigs are supposed to be there. Perhaps you and I stop by and learn some names and faces. Might be pertinent to your, ah, success."

"Babe, perhaps you weren't listening. I've been fired from this case. I've been handed a restraining order, I've been told to walk away, I've been threatened at gunpoint, and this morning I was shot at."

She gave me a look of disdain as she finished preparing her soup.

"And that means you're quitting?"

"Good point."

"That's better. What about this high school stud?"

"He bothers me. I didn't push him that hard at school, just asked a couple questions. Matter of fact, he tried to push me. No reason for him to go running to Dad for a restraining order."

"Means he's nervous."

"At least doesn't want me nosing around him."

"Think he's hiding something?"

"Kid as arrogant as Tommy is too used to everyone doing what he says. He's not normally prone to asking anyone for help, especially someone from a higher authority. Hurts his image and his pride."

"He's scared. Good. Looks like tomorrow is planned as well."

"Ms. Cassidy, I have been told by a very prominent police lieutenant to 'cease and desist any and all association' with one Tommy Banks. Are you suggesting that I break the law?"

"We, Samuel," she said, picking up the empty cartons. "We."

You had to love the girl.

The evening news had a little blurb on the shooting at Stanchion's office, which it reported as "thought to be somehow related to Michael Stanchion's bid for governor, probably from a deranged individual." The police were investigating, and life would go on as we knew it. Nowhere in the report was I mentioned. Neither were any prominent mobsters.

Lil made some calls to her clients while I cleaned up the kitchen, and then we settled in on the couch. One of the local radio stations was running a tribute to eighties heavy metal, which we could listen to, Lil said, as long as I understood we would never have sex again over the span of the next fifteen years. She had a wonderful way of explaining things so I could understand them, and we compromised by switching to some boxing matches that were being aired over an AM channel. Lil got some work done for the next day, and I read the newspaper. When the fights were over, we locked up, turned off the lights, went to my bedroom, and went to sleep.

22

I found the Bates' home address in the phone book, which if nothing else served to reinforce my faith in my own detective abilities. It was Friday, and Friday night by everything short of a state law was deemed the teenagers' night to play. I guessed that Tommy would stay after school and practice a bit, but would definitely come home and change before going out. Which is why, at four thirty, Lil and I were sitting in my car two houses down from Tommy's. It was a residential neighborhood, with houses lined up right next to each other, and while cars were not parked on the street in abundance, there were enough so that we didn't look out of the ordinary. Besides, the days were getting shorter, and by 4:30 the sun had already gone down and the streetlights were beginning to come on.

"I gotta tell you, Sam, you really know how to show a girl a good time. Friday night, and I'm sitting in a car staking out a teenager's house. I am definitely letting you get to second base later on."

"Don't be an asshole, babe. This was your idea."

"I realize that. And you are losing major points for saying 'I told you so.'"

While we waited for Tommy to get his act together and appear, we let the conversation drift over various terrain, some familiar and some not so much. We discussed what would constitute an ideal evening out, and even though we had been with each other for some time and had had these discussions before, it was fun revisiting old conversations and seeing how we had changed and what had remained the same.

We had often visualized the ideal double date with Everett and Nicole and surmised again that, if given the opportunity, Everett would get decked out in full tuxedo regalia, replete with white gloves and a cane, and would pick up Nicole in the most resplendent limousine imaginable. Nicole of course would be attired in nothing less than an evening gown that would make Ralph Lauren drool, wearing diamonds that glittered long into the night. They would dine at the most elegant of restaurants in the city of Boston, enjoying their meal on the top floor of the Prudential building and savoring the view of the city while they ate.

Everett would treat her to an elegant six-course meal, and the atmosphere would be complete with a twelve-piece orchestra playing in the background. After the meal, Everett would take Nicole out on the balcony to gaze at the stars and the lights of the city below. Eventually their gaze would fall on a tiny dive of a tavern embedded in one of the alleyways beneath them, and around midnight they would catch a glimpse of Lil and me being thrown out of said dive for reasons unknown but easily imagined, whereupon the two of them would make room at their table for us to join them for last call. The perfect end to the perfect evening.

Lil gave a stately giggle every time we told this story and would always finish by focusing her lovely green eyes fully on me and saying, "You do know that ten times out of ten I would rather be thrown out of a dive with you than enjoy the finest meal in the city with anyone else." Given that with her charm, wit, and natural beauty she could have literally anyone else but instead chose to walk by my side, that was no small comment. She leaned over and gave me a kiss, and I rested my hand on her thigh.

Finally at quarter of six, Tommy came out of his house and walked down his front steps. He was wearing a sweater, khakis, and deck shoes, and looked like he was going on a photo shoot for Abercrombie & Fitch. I would bet my entire

Guns N Roses collection that if we rolled down the window the distinctive aroma of Brut cologne would be lingering heavily in the air.

Daddy had lent Tom the keys to the Camry tonight, and he backed the car out of the driveway and headed off to his evening destination. We let him get to the second stop sign before putting the car in gear and pulling out behind him. He turned his car onto Route 108 and drove back towards the center of town.

At the first light he stopped off at a McDonalds and picked up some food at the drive-through. He passed through three more stoplights and turned into the Super Stop and Shop parking lot. He parked and went inside, returning momentarily with a bundle of roses. He didn't make it half a block down the street before he turned into a Mobil station to put gas in the car. Tommy was definitely not a plan-ahead type of guy. I pulled around to the back of a convenience store, and Lil ran in and bought a bag of peanuts. When she settled back into the car she said she was now prepared to sit back and enjoy what had the potential to be a very long show.

Tommy finished filling his car with gas, paid the attendant, and pulled back out into traffic. We followed easily. It was Friday night, traffic was active, it was dark, and there were two lanes. Plus, Tommy was a kid. If a seventeen-year-old was knowledgeable enough to notice he was being followed, we had bigger issues than I was prepared to deal with.

He bore to the right off the rotary and headed back towards the water. Halfway down the street he turned left into the driveway for Crispin Fields, a large recreational park that included a baseball diamond and soccer fields. We coasted to the side of the road and turned off our lights. When the traffic cleared, we turned down the driveway and stopped about halfway down. It was the end of October. No one was in the mood for tennis. Because the cold weather rendered the park pretty much useless, most of it was unlit, leaving it blanketed in darkness. Lil and I sat unnoticed in the dark and watched as Tommy drove down into the parking lot. There was one other car, illuminated under the sole streetlight in the lot, and he pulled up alongside it. While Lil reached into her bag and popped some peanuts in her mouth, Tommy got out of his car and into the passenger side of the second one.

"Cue the suspenseful music," Lil said as she munched.

"Two cars in an abandoned parking lot on a Friday night. I'm guessing drugs or sex."

"He brought flowers," Lil pointed out. "It's sex."

We sat there for a little over ten minutes. When I was pretty sure all pleasantries had been exchanged and Tommy had gotten down to the business of the night with his friend in the car, I left Lil with her peanuts and got out of the car.

"Don't block my view," Lil said as I shut the door.

I thought back to nights in high school when you drove around all night trying to find a secluded spot nobody else had staked out yet. I thought about the idiocy of bucket seats from a teenager's perspective, and I remembered Megan Kulley's constant complaint that the steering wheel always cut into the small of her back.

I wasn't sure exactly what I hoped to accomplish by sneaking up on Tommy. Hopefully by catching him in a potentially awkward situation I could scare him enough to let him know I wasn't staying away, but hold enough leverage that he wouldn't want to run and complain to the police. That was the hope, anyway. A small part of me thought I could go to jail for coming across two kids in the middle of some lewd act, but Lil was my witness, and in a worst-case scenario we could always claim we heard someone yell for help and went to investigate.

The windows were fogged over when I came to the car. Points to Lil. I reached for the car door handle and actually heard "suspenseful music" in the back of my head, damn her. The moment of truth. I gripped the handle and pulled the door open. Inside the car I found a half-naked Ms. Gloria Hurdtz wrapped around a shirtless-and-soon-to-be-completely-naked Tommy Bates. I smiled down graciously at the two of them as they looked up at me.

"Glory be," I said.

23

Last February

Tommy Bates picked a towel up off the bench and mopped his head. He felt the chill on his body he felt at the end of every game, an ephemeral feeling that let him know the game was over. He looked over at the scoreboard one last time: 118 to 84. Not bad. The Wildcats were supposed to be the second-best team in the league. Tommy's team had shut their point guard down early and used just enough fouls to incapacitate their starting center. After that, the second half had been a piece of cake. If this was any indication of how the season would go, Tommy's team basically had undisputed access to go all the way this year.

Tommy's team. Of course officially his team was called the Sea Dogs, but that was just a formality. It really was "Tommy's Team." Ask any of the kids in school, the regular news reporters, and even a few of the opposing coaches. They'd all agree: Unofficially, the real name of this team was "Tommy's Team."

And why the hell not? Shit, it's not like this was an ego thing. He wasn't a ball hog or a glory hound. He simply knew how to work his team on the court. He orchestrated the ball to his teammates flawlessly, played rough defense, and had an unnatural outside shot. And he knew this game. He was smart. Even his coach asked his opinion in the huddle.

No, it wasn't an ego thing, but no one would deny that this was Tommy's team. Tommy loved this game. He played hard. And that passion transferred to his teammates on the court and to the fans in the crowd. Coming to a home game was electric; it was a rock concert. The energy was tangible, and the conduit for that energy was Tommy Bates. He created it, he fueled it, and he sent it out to everyone.

Some leaders worked quietly behind the scenes, and some were loud and right at the center of everything. Tommy didn't ask for it; it just happened that way. People asked for leadership, and he answered them, becoming a king in his own castle along the way.

Tommy turned to the bleachers and watched the people emptying out. The librarian, Ms. Hurdtz, smiled and waved at him. Tommy smiled back, as much to himself as to her. It had become the undisputed collective agreement of the junior class that Ms. Hurdtz was definitely the hottest teacher in the school.

Granted, she had a leg up on the competition already—the next youngest teacher wasn't even born in the same decade—but Jesus Christ, look at her! OK, her tits were a little small, but everything she wore put 'em on display, her ass was fine, and her legs were absolutely smokin'. Even now as she descended the bleachers step by step, Tommy figured he could pop some wood just looking at her legs. As a matter of fact, the first thing Tommy noticed was that her skirt was cut short enough to showcase as much leg as possible.

The second thing Tommy noticed was she was walking straight down towards him.

"Hi, Tommy," she said as she stepped off the bleachers and onto the gym floor. She smiled brilliantly at him and pushed her blond hair back behind her ear. "That was a great game you played."

She wore a white button-down blouse with a silver necklace and a jean skirt that looked even shorter up close.

"Thanks, Ms. Hurdtz," Tommy replied.

"Oh please, Tommy," she said, still smiling. "We're not in school right now. Call me Gloria."

Tommy smiled back at her.

"That really was a good game." She reached out and playfully stroked his shoulder. "You're quite a player."

"Thank you," Tommy said. He couldn't quite get around to calling her Gloria, but he didn't want to look like a dumb kid and keep calling her Ms. Hurdtz. "We all try to play real hard, y'know? The whole team."

"Yes, I know," Gloria agreed. "The team works very well together. You all play very hard." She glanced around the gym. "Well this place cleared out in a hurry, didn't it?"

Her smile was mesmerizing.

"It's a school night. On Friday nights, though, people usually hang out and go for pizza afterwards."

He winced. He had to be sounding like such a dork to her.

"Everybody's gone home already? Such good students. I don't think I was that good when I was in school." She laughed and looked around the gym again. "Do you have a team meeting or anything, Tommy?"

Tommy shook his head. "No."

"Would you like to go for some pizza? Celebrate your win?"

She turned back and smiled at him again.

"Uh, sure," Tommy managed to say without stammering. "Just let me take a quick shower."

"Make sure it's quick," Gloria Hurdtz said, sitting back down on the bleachers and crossing those gloriously long legs.

"I'll be right out," Tommy said.

"I'll be waiting right here."

Holy fuck, Tommy Bates thought as he walked into the boys' locker room. Holy fuck.

Tommy lunged out of the car at me. He was a reedy teenager to begin with and was already using one hand to pull up his pants, so he didn't present much of a fight. Gloria stumbled out of the car in her skirt, stuffing half of herself back into her bra, and tried to push in between the two of us. From the car I could hear Lil exclaim, "Ha! I was right!"

Tommy was still struggling against me. I grabbed his free arm and pulled it hard behind him and slammed him up against the car.

"Settle down, Tommy."

His other hand was still gripping the top of his pants, and if he wanted to fight back, he'd have to drop his pants, which he was reluctant to do. Ah, pride. I cast a look towards Gloria, who was still disheveled and not quite as enticing as she had looked the previous afternoon.

"You might want to put yourself back together."

"I want to make sure you don't hurt him," she said.

Lil, being Lil, chose that moment to turn on the headlights of the Mustang, bathing the three of us in incandescent high-beam light. Gloria rethought her stance and slunk back to the driver's side to get dressed.

"You are in so much shit, man," Tommy said. "My dad will have the police throw your ass in jail."

"Good point, Tommy," I said. I took my cell phone out of my pocket. "Let's get your father down here right now."

Gloria's head appeared over the top of the car. "What?"

Lil had gotten out of the car and walked down to us. She was wearing a brown suede jacket and cowgirl boots that crunched on the broken asphalt as she walked. "Evening, all," she said. Gloria looked at her, then back at me. Even in the crisp fall air she looked a bit pale. Lil continued walking until she was standing next to Gloria, who was half in and half out of the car and looking remarkably like a deer on speed caught in headlights. Lil crossed her arms and leaned against the car.

"Don't even think about going anywhere, sweetie."

Everybody looked at everybody. Nobody said anything.

"Well?" I finally asked. "We've caught you, Tommy, quite literally with your pants down. And Gloria, this has the potential to be quite the topic of conversation at the next PTA meeting. I'm pretty sure it's illegal for you to be having sex with him even if he does have a library card."

"What do you want?" Gloria asked. Her voice was tiny.

For a moment she had me stumped. It was a good question. What did I want? I wanted to hear that Tommy Bates killed Jessica Stanchion so I could crush his larynx and feel justified. I looked across the roof of the car. Gloria's face was frozen. Her eyes were pleading for a way out of this mess.

"I want answers," I said. Keep it vague and see what they give you.

"Dude," Tommy barked. "I already tol—"

"Shut up," I said and leaned in on his arm.

"Don't hurt him," Gloria said, her voice regaining strength in the form of a whine.

"He's just gruff darlin'," Lil said. "His bark is much worse than his bite. Trust me." She touched the tip of her finger to Gloria's chin and steered it over to her line of vision. Gloria didn't fight; she let Lil direct her. Her fists were clenched up by her throat. Lil took Gloria's hands in hers and gently guided them down. She smiled. Sweet Auntie Lil. "How did this girl die?"

"I don't know," Gloria said. Her eyes were still wide. "The poor thing was shot. We just woke up one morning and the newspapers—Ow! Ow!! What are you doing?" Gloria didn't quite yell, but she did seem to get shorter as she buckled from a little undue pressure given by Lil. "Let go of my hands!"

That's my girl.

Lil continued to smile. As far as she was concerned we were roasting marshmallows around a campfire singing choir hymns.

"Give us a better answer than that please, Gloria."

"Really—Ow!—the last time we saw her was at Tommy's. She came over and caught us in bed together and ran away crying. That was it! Owww!"

Gloria's speech became quicker with each passing word and her height seemed to diminish to where I could barely see her over the car. Lil held her a moment longer and then let her go. I heard a sob catch in her throat as she stood up. I couldn't see, but I was sure she was rubbing her wrists where Lil had pressed in on her.

Lil came around the back of the car. I had Tommy against the car so his head was turned to the left. She looked at Tommy.

"Please don't let us find anything new on our own," she said.

I fought the urge to say "or we'll be back" and let Tommy go. Lil and I walked away. Before we reached the Mustang we heard one car door slam behind us and an engine start up. By the time the two of us were in my car, Gloria's Jetta was driving past us.

I turned the engine over.

"So, what, you're my partner now?" I asked.

"Always."

"You got more answers than I did. Keep it up and you'll start bruising my ego."

Bates pealed, as much as a Camry can peal, out of the parking lot and sped past us, flipping us off I'm sure, in the process. Poor Gloria didn't even get her flowers.

"You just didn't threaten the right person, that's all."

How nice to be sitting next to such the voice of experience.

How even nicer to be dating her.

No one was waiting to arrest us when we came home, and there was no phone call from an irate police department the following morning. Obviously Gloria had thought it prudent not to complain to the police about being manhandled—or womanhandled—while she was in the middle of molesting one of her adolescent students from the high school. Round of applause to her.

The event, however, was still not as productive as one might have hoped. I still had no motive for Jessica's death, my suspect list seemed to be dwindling, and all I was left with was the annoying revelation that librarians were apparently much more fun than I remembered growing up. Oh yes, let's not forget that I was also no longer getting paid.

Which is why, at three o'clock the following afternoon, Lil and I were sitting in the parking lot of Cranston's luxurious Royal Arms hotel, watching people come and go from Stanchion's fundraiser reception. The rain had returned at a slow pace, and the wipers hummed intermittently across the windshield, cleansing and recleansing our view.

We were parked off to the side of the lot, with a full view of the entrance. There was only one, albeit large, driveway by which one could gain entrance to the hotel, and as such no one could come and go without our noticing. The groundskeepers earned their pay at the Royal Arms, the driveway alone requiring more attention than a golf course. Neatly manicured, the half-mile stretch was adorned on either side by countless flower arrangements of all shapes and sizes, while the greenery itself stretched off widely in both directions.

"This is the second day in a row I've spent in a car with you," observed Lil.

"Speaks volumes about your loyalty," I said.

"It also marks the longest stretch of time I've been in a parked car and kept my clothes on."

"Good to know. Perhaps we'll change that later."

"Bucket seats, pal. No chance."

We sat watching through the rain as people came and went through the revolving doors. Stanchion and his wife had arrived earlier, but the parade of people making an appearance was steady and people came and went continuously. Everyone was well dressed. Everyone waited in their cars until a doorman came over with an umbrella. Everyone smiled in case a news photographer was lurking around the corner. This was politics.

At three forty-one, a familiar black Lincoln skated through the puddles and parked, and the goomba who broke into my house pushed himself out of the car. He was attired in a three-piece suit that came complete with a gold chain across the vest. Where he found clothing of that style for his size was beyond me. He lumbered across the parking lot while the attendant hurried to keep up with him and struggled to reach him with the umbrella. He came alone but nodded to the doorman with the same familiarity with which he treated everybody.

"Finally, someone I know," I said, pointing him out.

"He the one who took you off the case?" asked Lil.

I nodded.

"Great. I'll get us a picture."

Before I could say anything she was out of the car and striding into the hotel. I sat in the car, drummed my fingers on the steering wheel, and listened to the motor run. Within ten minutes Lil walked out of the hotel and back into the car.

"You brought a camera with you?"

She shook her head. "Phone."

"You called a photographer?"

"No asshole. My phone has a camera."

She pulled her cell phone out of her raincoat pocket and flipped it open. On her screen was a very clear image of the sumo wrestler who had fired me. She scrolled down and showed me three more, one a very engaging left profile.

"That's awesome," I said.

"Yeah, your phone has the same feature, babe."

Sonofabitch.

My attention was drawn to the revolving door, where I was witness to four very large but well-dressed men walking out of the hotel and quite hastily over to us. One of the gentlemen just happened to be the one Lil photographed.

"Think anyone saw you take the pictures?" I asked.

"Perhaps."

The four men surrounded the front of the car, two of them standing directly in front, one of them coming over to the passenger side, and my large friend, of course, coming over to my side. I hit the button to lock the doors and rolled my window down enough to speak.

"Good afternoon," I said.

"Mr. Miller," said Gorilla. "I'm surprised to see you. I thought we had an agreement." He looked past me at Lil. "Your lady friend took some pictures. Give us the phone."

"Do you have any idea how much those phones cost?"

"Give us the phone, Mr. Miller. This is no time for levity."

The two goons in front of the car leaned in and placed their hands on the hood. The one on the passenger side looked increasingly uncomfortable in the rain. Gorilla didn't seem to notice. His eyes fixated on mine.

"The phone."

Lil crossed her legs and rested her hands on her knee. I gave Gorilla a sad look. He tried to open the door. I floored the Mustang in reverse and spun around. The two who had been leaning on the hood sprawled forward. The guy on Lil's side fell back into a bush. Gorilla didn't move. He just watched as we sped down the driveway and into traffic.

26

Last April

Michael brought the drinks in and placed them on the hotel dresser. The girl, Runter's latest gift, came out of the bathroom drying her hair with a towel. Corey had been very generous with his girls. Gave Michael first pick, free of charge, every time. This one had short hair that curled below her ears, and small breasts. Michael handed her one of the drinks. She took it with a smile and settled into one of the two leather armchairs in the room.

Michael watched her, fascinated. He had gotten to know Runter's whores more and more as his campaign gained steam, and he had become entranced by them. He was awed by their chameleon-like abilities, able to become whatever it was you wanted, knowing what it was you wanted them to be. Moments ago Marilyn had been his passage into a wondrous ecstasy. Now, sitting there across from him, her face freshly scrubbed clean of all her makeup, she looked like a fragile little girl.

"Do you like your...job, Marilyn?" he ventured.

"My job?" she smiled.

Her voice squeaked out of her.

For a moment Michael looked at her and wondered if she were much older than his own daughter.

"Pays the bills," she said. "Keeps me in these places." She waved her hand in a circle, recognizing the ornate furnishings of the suite Michael had for the weekend. "Gets me nice clothes and stuff. But it's not really that glamorous."

Glamorous? Michael thought. "Why not?" he asked, intrigued.

"Well, it's not like you can pick your clientele. I mean, you're OK," she quickly added, "but some of these guys, well...if you need a whore there must be a reason why, right?"

She shrugged her shoulders and made small circles in her drink with her straw. She shifted her weight in the chair, and her robe fell open, exposing her breast. Michael stared at the soft, pink flesh. Marilyn either didn't notice or didn't care.

"Would you rather do something else?" Michael asked.

"Not much else I can do. Nothing that would keep me in this kind of place." Again, the hand wave.

"The money must be pretty good," Michael said in a conciliatory tone. "I know what Mr. Runter charges his clients."

"And he keeps most of what he gets. We don't see it. For all the cash changing hands, we're still on an hourly wage." Marilyn sipped her drink. She looked up at Michael. "I don't mean to sound angry. I know the two of you are friends."

"We're business associates," Michael said. Again the fatherly tone. Why the fatherly tone to a whore? "Don't worry."

Marilyn nodded. "Wouldn't matter anyway. If Corey's angry at something, he'll find a way to take it out on one of us, one way or another."

"He beats you?"

"Nothing visible. Can't damage the merchandise, or there's nothing to sell." She took a long pull on her drink. "He's cracked ribs. Given kidney punches to put us down and remind us of our place." She finished her drink and placed it on the nightstand. *"We actually thought about fighting back once."* She nestled herself into a ball in the chair. *"Almost tried to have him killed. There's this shooter. Name of Max. The best. You want someone taken care of, he's the man. Pay in cash at this bar Mulligan's, and you're all set. No one sees Max come or go. No mess, no trace, problem solved. We almost went about hiring Max to kill Corey."*

"What happened?"

"We took a look around. Corey's the reason we get into places like this. Without him, we'd all be fighting each other for a place on the street." She stopped for a moment and looked at herself in the mirror. *"We need Corey. A couple of punches are OK now and then, as long as we stay in business."*

The life of a whore, Michael thought to himself. He wondered if Corey thought Michael needed him to stay in business. That would be a very foolish thought indeed. He looked back over at Marilyn curled up in the opposite corner of the room, so fragile, so vulnerable.

"Want to go at it again, Marilyn?" he asked.

"Actually, my name's not even Marilyn," she answered.

"What is it?"

"It's Sally."

"I like Marilyn."

Sally looked up and met his eyes briefly. She smiled thinly.

"Of course you do."

"Want to go at it again?"

"Sure." She took off her robe. *"Why not? You own me for the rest of the afternoon."*

27

"Horace Zile," Lieutenant Simon said, looking at the pictures on Lil's phone. "Works with Seamus Lynch."

We had killed time with a long dinner and a late movie while waiting for Lucille's shift to begin. While we walked over to her desk, Lil reminded me that our first date had ended in a police station as well. Ah, history.

"Who's Seamus Lynch?"

"Mob boss. What the movies would call the 'patriarch' of organized crime in Rhode Island, although lately he seems to have limited himself mainly to the drug trade."

"You know all this and he's not in jail?"

"You want me to help you on this or not?"

"Sorry."

"Have we pieced together the big picture? Yes. Can we prove anything? No. Witnesses die or get cold feet and change their story on the stand. We pick up carriers with the stuff who point fingers, but Lynch keeps himself clean from association. It's not like we're not busting our asses; but again, we can't just throw anyone in jail we feel like."

"OK, sorry."

"Horace is one of Lynch's bagmen. Transports bags of money for him. None of the shit, just cash. We've picked him up a few times, but he never has anything on him but money. Can't book him for carrying around thousands of dollars in a suitcase. We can just watch where he carries it to."

"Seamus Lynch and Corey Runter have anything to do with each other?"

"How do you know Runter?"

"Homework."

"They're business partners. Basically, Runter makes sure anyone south of Boston has to go to Providence to deal in the drug trade. Guarantees Lynch a monopoly. Lynch, in turn, assures Runter that any prostitutes for Rhode Island are 'imported' through him."

"That's bullshit," I said. "I know there are pimps in Rhode Island."

"Of course there are. And they all pay a weekly stipend to Corey Runter. Any girl tries to work outside the stable and she is forced into an 'early retirement.'"

Holy shit. I was starting to need an MBA to understand police work.

"How do you know all this?"

"Informants. Like I said; we pick up somebody, they cop a plea and roll over for some information. You scare enough people and hear enough of the same story, you piece together a picture." She stopped for a minute and looked at me. "Isn't this your line of work?"

"Yeah, it is. I just wanted to know how you do it."

"How do you do it?"

"Usually I beg. Although lately I've been relying on her." I gestured at Lil who smiled politely.

Lucille closed her eyes and pinched the bridge of her nose. "I have work to do."

We stood up to leave.

"I assume you'll be staying at her place for awhile?" she said, nodding towards Lil.

I shook my head.

"Sam, he knows where you live."

"Exactly. I don't need him knowing where she lives too."

She smiled to herself.

"Chivalry."

"It's not dead."

"Just make sure you're not either."

"Lieutenant Simon, I didn't know you cared."

"I don't. But I have enough work to do here. I don't need your death adding to it."

With those words of encouragement at our back, Lil and I stepped out into the quiet of the early, early morning. I took her hand as we descended the front steps.

"If I recall, our first date didn't quite end at the police station."

"No?"

"I believe I took you back to your hotel room where we made mad, passionate love into the wee hours of the morning."

Lil's eyes flickered with a mischief I could see in the darkness.

"In your dreams, Samuel."

As hard as it is to believe, Lil does have a life outside of me, and the next morning she had to return to it. We returned home very late, or very early in the morning, and she got less than the minimal amount of sleep, which was sure to have a profound affect on her mood. A part of me felt sorry for her first client. A larger part of me was annoyed at actually having to work on my case myself.

I had some leftover Chinese food in the fridge, which sufficed as my Sunday morning breakfast. I cleaned the leftover dishes in the sink and straightened up the rest of the house. If my detective business continued to plummet, perhaps I could make it as a housecleaner. Thankfully, serious pursuit of that endeavor was interrupted shortly after ten with the ringing of my phone.

"Samuel," Everett said after I answered. "I e-mailed you a folder of documents on Michael Stanchion. It mostly details his campaign, but as that was the majority of information available, that substantiated what I was able to accumulate."

"It's more than I have right now," I said. I added after a moment, "Don't you guys ever sleep?"

"I do," he answered. "Not my staff."

I thanked him and hung up.

My computer was basically a makeshift construction of a laptop with external speakers and a separate printer. I had bought the speakers so I could listen to radio stations that broadcast over the Internet. They were top-of-the-line quality. My printer, conversely, was covered in a film of dust. Priorities.

I sat down at my desk and accessed my e-mail. Everett was very resourceful and rarely wasteful. If he sent anything, he would send it because he thought it would raise my awareness levels in matters of import. Those were his words. I was just hoping for something useful.

It took me over two hours to sift through all the material Everett collected. The files mainly consisted of photos and press releases of various campaign functions Stanchion either attended or hosted, and he was pictured standing with a multitude of local dignitaries and minor celebrities. Horace did a good job of avoiding the camera and wasn't found in any of the shots, but a regular cast of characters soon became apparent as I scanned through the photos.

Stanchion dominated most of the photos, adorned in a dark suit and robust smile, and most of the time he was flanked on either side by two men identified as Peter Siddick, his campaign manager, and Simon Malone, his fundraising chair. Brains and money; Stanchion didn't travel without either of them close by his side.

His wife was pictured in roughly half the shots, always right by his side and embodying the picture of wholesome family goodness. Other pictures contained a tall, attractive woman, impeccably dressed, with a gleaming smile, who also looked to be a good twenty years younger than Mrs. Vanessa Stanchion.

A quick review of the pictures showed that the two women never attended the same functions, or at least were never in the same photo together. This second woman, however, was always at Stanchion's side, more often than not resting a hand on his arm or shoulder while she smiled at the camera. Siddick, Malone, and Mrs. Stanchion were always listed by name, but the tall lovely one was continually referred to simply as "campaign staff."

Ignoring all the obvious jokes about campaign contributions as best I could, I came to the only logical conclusion an ingenious private investigator such as myself would: Campaign staff my ass. Michael Stanchion had a sweetie on the side.

Last May

"My name's Erin."

The woman strode forward confidently, extending her hand to Michael Stanchion as she did so. She was attired professionally in an off-white dress that buttoned straight up the back and wore matching stockings and pumps. She had rich, luxurious golden-blond hair that fell to the top of her shoulders, and a pair of blue and yellow earrings dangled from her ears and seemed to shimmer in the lights.

"Pleased to meet you," Michael said, shaking her hand. She had a firm, strong grip and looked him straight in the eye.

"I want to work for you."

"I beg your pardon?" He stepped back for a moment and regarded her. She stood proudly erect and crossed her arms in front of her.

"I want to work for you," she repeated.

"Just like that, huh?" he laughed.

"Just like that," she smiled.

"Well, Miss..."

"Oregot. Erin Oregot."

"*Well, Miss Oregot, we can always use more help, especially from someone as lovely as yourself, but what exactly would you do? Did you plan on bringing something specific to the table?*"

"*Public relations.*"

"*Public relations. I see. No offense meant, Miss Oregot—*"

"*Erin.*"

"*No offense meant, Erin, but if you take a look around at our clientele, I think you'll see we have the public relations aspect well in hand here.*"

"*That's exactly why I've brought three new businesses in to see you about donating some substantial campaign funds. Now if you'll walk with me over to this corner table...*"

Erin took Michael by the arm and led him over in the direction where three men sat waiting for him. Michael let her guide him. He let her wrap her fingers around his bicep and told himself she was simply taking him to another business meeting. Another cog in the machine, that's all.

Michael drank in her perfume as she escorted him across the room. He gave her a sideways glance and almost lost himself in the nape of her neck. She saw him look and gave him a half-smile in return.

OK, Miss Erin Oregot, he thought to himself, you're hired.

OK, Miss Erin Oregot. Looks like you'll be around for awhile.

The seaport of Galilee is a small community located in Narragansett's Point Judith. It's an old-fashioned fishing village that started somewhere back in the eighteenth century and, like the shark, hasn't had to evolve much since its creation. Tall-masted ships still dock at the piers, the pungent odor of fish is still strong in the air, and the population is still made up of burly, hardworking people. It's a good place.

There's a misconception that the docks are overrun with people trafficking in a variety of corrupt dealings. That's not entirely true. Sure, there are plenty of illegal goods being transported off the boats, and yes, if you wander around, you'll more than likely find someone you can hire to perform almost any type of underground activity. But the docks are also filled with down-to-earth laborers trying to scrape out a living. Graham Porter falls into the latter category.

He's been in his share of scraps, sure. He associates with people you wouldn't invite to your sister's wedding, absolutely. But if you're choosing up sides, Graham is a man you want on your team.

Anyone who spends more than a day in Galilee knows Graham. He's a tough one to miss. His figure's the size of an upright, mutated ox, and people unconsciously move out of the way as he lugs crates and barrels up and down the street from the boats to the shops and back. With a watch cap covering his bald head and gold hoops hanging from each of his earlobes, all he'd have to do is sing "Yo Ho, Yo Ho" and he'd be a shoo-in for a job at Disneyland.

Once in a while you'll catch him riding around town on his Harley, but for the most part he stays right in Galilee. He sleeps on the docks and showers on one of the boats that's docked in the morning. He eats in the local taverns, and when it gets cold, he rents a room in one of the two hotels that do next to nothing in terms of business in the off-season anyway.

Galilee is his home, and he is its surrogate protector. Nothing happens on the docks that Graham doesn't know about. And nothing happens on the docks that he doesn't approve. If you need information, or anything else for that matter, Graham is the man to go to.

I got there at nine o'clock at night, and while the darkness might hamper your vision, the sounds were startlingly crisp in the air, especially over the water. The ferry to Block Island had made its last run an hour before, and the road was pretty much empty of tourists and vacationing families. Two bars at the end of the street were vibrant with noise and music, but for once in my life a drink was not what I was after. I parked the car and walked back in the other direction toward the pier. The fishing was done for the day, but the docks were still bristling with activity.

The only light at the docks came from the stars overhead and the occasional passing car. If you were lucky you might find a sole lantern hanging on a post, but I wouldn't count on it. The people on the pier at night knew what they were doing and knew where they were going. Either you belonged there or you didn't.

I walked amongst the docks until I found what I was looking for. A large, hulking figure was stacking crates at the end of the pier. He moved with the rhythm of the tide, back and forth, slowly, methodically, purposefully. He belonged there; he was as much a part of Galilee as the creaking of the docks and the scrape of the boats against the buoys.

"Graham Porter," I said into the darkness.

The silhouette stacked one more crate and stopped. I could see him lean forward as if peering out to see who was there. I stepped into the light of a streetlamp to give him a better view.

"Sam," he growled back at me. "Been awhile. Business or pleasure?"

"Business," I said.

"Step outta the light."

I obliged him and stepped onto the pier. My hand was gripped in what felt like an iron shovel as Graham shook my hand in greeting and led me over to an abandoned crate on which I sat. He lit a cigarette, and his forearms resembled two beer kegs as they flashed in the glow from his butane lighter. He clicked off the lighter and I could smell the smoke drift out through the night air.

"You been the talk o' the town the last week." Graham's voice was like coal slowly smoldering away in the fire. "Coupla people startin' t'become highly irritated wit' the fact that you breathin' so easily."

"Hard to believe isn't it?"

Graham laughed. "I think the best line I heard was, 'Shoot him in the chest. He doesn't have any brains to blow out.'"

"I'm sure you stood up for me."

"I'm not gonna embarrass myself. Although I did turn down the opportunity t'submerge ya fer an extended period of time an' watch you die."

"That was nice of you."

"You don't have many friends. I felt sorry for you."

"Loyalty."

Graham laughed again. "Not really. You don't want t'know what dey wuz offerin' to pay fer your, ah, termination."

"Never said I was worth much."

"Got that right."

"So who's looking to have me knocked off? Corey Runter?"

"Now you're not givin' yourself enough credit. Two guys came down here three days ago, scoutin' around, lookin' to find somebody to take you out. You known well enough around here that it piques people's interest enough to come out and take a look to see who's askin' and see if it's worth their while."

"Nice to know people care."

"I said you were known. Didn't say you wuz liked. Anyway, word gets around, and somebody talks to somebody who talks to somebody who talks to somebody else, and it turns out word came down from the big man himself, Seamus Lynch."

The waves lapped the dock as Graham took a drag on his cigarette.

"Look at me," I said, after a moment. "I made the big leagues. Really wasn't that hard.'"

"What'd you do?"

"Went back to high school. By way of Michael Stanchion."

"Stanchion. You are in the big leagues."

"So I've learned. You feel like watching my back for a little while?"

"If you're in with Lynch and Stanchion, you're gonna need it."

"What's the cost?"

The wind blew in off the water and Graham's dying cigarette glowed red for a moment.

"This one's on the house. I'm still ticked off over how little they offered t'dump you."

"Stick around. Price might go up."

"Good to know," he said. "What's the first course of action?"

"We're going to go knocking on Seamus Lynch's door."

Graham's laugh was hoarse and flat. He threw his cigarette butt into the water and stood up.

"They were right when they said not to waste bullets on yer head."

The floorboards creaked as he turned and walked off into the blackness.

In retrospect, I probably should have retained Graham's services right from the start, but I had more important issues on my mind. I was starving. It was past ten, and the only thing I had eaten all day was leftover Chinese. Refrigerated Moo Goo Gai Pan didn't cut it as an all-day feast.

There was a local market that stayed open until midnight, and I pulled into the parking lot on my way home. It was ten thirty on a Sunday and as such only two cashiers were on, but I had a deal with the butcher, and he put a few cuts of steak aside for me every couple of weeks. The check Stanchion had written me for a retainer had cleared, and I figured I ought to spend as much of it as I could before he asked for it back.

One of the workers was mopping the floors, and the overhead lights reflecting off the white tile contrasted greatly with the empty night outside. The girl working the counter wrapped my purchase in thick white paper, and I paid for my food and walked out through the automatic doors into the parking lot.

"Mr. Miller," a voice said to the side of me as I walked out.

"Yep," I said and kept walking towards my car.

"Mr. Miller, we need to talk," the voice said, coming up beside me and matching my stride. It was a high, thin voice that almost seemed to have trouble cutting through the air.

"I doubt it," I said as I reached my car. The glow from one of the lights in the parking lot produced an incandescent circle that filtered through the darkness. I opened my door, placed my meat inside, pulled out my gun, and turned around and pointed it at the voice. "The way I've been treated in the last few days, anyone following me around at night and then telling me we need to talk is probably not in my best interests."

"I beg to differ," the voice said, and a figure appeared in the half-light. He was about my height, dressed in an overcoat, and wore a scarf and gloves even though the temperature hadn't dropped below sixty. He had short hair that was light in color, and a big nose.

"Corey Runter."

His mouth split into a wolfish grin and he spread his arms wide as he finished closing the gap between us.

"Samuel Miller. I suppose I shouldn't be flattered you recognize me. From what I've been told you're pretty thorough." He paused for a minute and cocked his head to one side as if he were appraising me. "Put the gun down, Samuel. I'm not armed. I just want to talk."

"My ears are free," I said, and leaned my back against my car and leveled my gun at his chest.

"Suit yourself," he shrugged. He looked down at the ground as if he were collecting his thoughts. Four cars drove past the parking lot, their headlights trained on the road in front of them.

"Do you know how important you should feel that I've traveled down from Massachusetts personally to see you?" He pressed his gloved hands together and brought them up to his lips. He raised his eyes back towards me.

"You had no choice," I replied. "I've seen your hired help. You need to upgrade your personnel."

Runter's chuckle sounded like chipped ice. "Yes, perhaps you're right," he said. His grin still split across his face like a demonic clown. He paused again, like a theatre major, breathing slowly and easily, biding his time and choosing his words. He had all the time in the world. I, of course, was still hungry.

"You have an impressive background, Mr. Miller," he resumed. "Congressional accolades, U.S. Marshals...it causes one to wonder why you have chosen this particular path. Do you know how much money a man of your talents could stand to make under me?"

"That shit's old, Mr. Runter. Your man Horace already tried to buy me off."

"He offered cash. I'm offering employment."

The night air was still. The lighting was dim. We stood there listening to each other's breathing.

"Am I correct in understanding that your silence means no?"

"Yep."

"Am I also correct in understanding, then, that you will not be willingly persuaded to walk away and leave well enough alone?"

"About as willing as you are to tell me why you're so eager to have me walk."

"I see." He spread his hands wide again and shrugged. "A pity."

Contrary to what you see in most low-budget horror movies, when the power goes out to trap the handsome hero, it doesn't flicker on and off. It just goes. And there's no "bzzzzzt"-like sound that accompanies it either. If anything, the silence just gets louder. I know this, because as I stood there in the parking lot with Corey Runter, the power went out. The lights in the parking lot, the lights on the storefront, the lights inside the store, everything. And of course, as I stood there drenched in the darkness, I was grabbed by roughly four arms and pinned against my car by what seemed to be hands made of solid rock.

Just once in my life I would like to not be the handsome hero.

I couldn't see Runter anymore, but his voice fell on me out of the night. "I was never a big fan of guns, Mr. Miller," I heard from a distance. "I always thought they seemed to stifle one's creativity." I heard his footsteps as he walked away. "Let me know if you still think I need to upgrade my help."

My last thought was I probably wouldn't get to cook my steak tonight.

And then everything went cold.

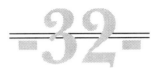

I awoke in a hospital room. I heard the motor of the oxygen tank first and then smelled the sterile antiseptic used to clean an already very sterile room. When I finally noticed the sunlight streaming in over my hospital bed, I was somewhat awake, and thus came to the realization that I was in a hospital. No slacker detective, I. I looked to my left, and Lucille Simon, wearing a green blouse and jeans, was sitting in a chair in the corner eating what I presumed to be my hospital food.

"Aren't you supposed to give that to the guy wearing the hospital gown?" I asked. I started to sit up, but a burning pain in my right side only allowed me to make it halfway.

"You're too weak. This food'll kill you."

"What happened?" I pushed myself up gingerly so I was sitting up straight. Nothing like good posture in a hospital gown.

"Power went out at Dellan's Market. One of the kids went around back to flip the breakers, and when she came around front she found you lying on the ground unconscious with a screwdriver stuck in your side."

"Phillips or flathead?"

"She pulled you inside, called 911, and put a compress on you to try to stop the bleeding. When that didn't work, she put you in the meat locker to slow your heart rate down until the ambulance arrived."

"She put me in the meat locker?"

"Saved your life."

"Why are you here?"

"Carlston gave me a call once he ID'd you, and I drove over."

"On your way to work?"

"My night off."

"Bartender?"

"I'll see him tomorrow."

I felt my side. It felt rough and plastered over like a half-assed spackle job. My intestines were not leaking out anywhere, and I took that as a good sign.

Lieutenant Simon opened a drawer by my bed.

"Your gun's in here. The girl found it on the ground when she pulled you in."

"That would be Christy."

"You're lucky. Lot of kids would've kept it for themselves."

"Mm-mm. She's a good girl. I tip her whenever I go to the market."

"You tip the cashier?"

"She's putting herself through college."

"You tip the cashier."

"Gas money."

Lucille stood up.

"I've put an officer outside your door. Let him know when you want to grace us with your presence and fill us in on the events that led up to you being stabbed with home improvement tools."

"Corey Runter," I murmured.

"Sam?" I heard Lucille ask, and then I faded out again.

The next time I woke up Lil was sitting in a chair next to my bed reading a magazine. She wore a yellow dress, her hair was down, and she had on her wire-rimmed glasses, which meant she had found an article actually worth reading and wasn't just idly flipping through to pass the time.

"It's about time," she smiled, as I pushed myself up.

"How long have you been here?"

"Long enough to make sure that the nurse giving you your sponge bath isn't that good-looking, which, incidentally, isn't as easy as it sounds."

"Sponge bath wouldn't take that long anyway. You know that."

"Lucky for her. Lucky for you too."

"That's only because you've seen her." I felt my side again. "What kind of shape am I in?"

"You've got fifty staples in your lower right side. You lost a lot of blood when you arrived, but no infections."

"Where's my car?"

"My place." She hesitated. "I'm not going to tell you what to do, Sam. But the doctor's not going to want you to go running around right away. You rip open your wound and you'll be worse off than when you started."

"Doctor can't tell me not to leave. I'll be careful."

Lil nodded to herself, reaffirming something she already knew.

"Lucille made it sound worse."

"She worries about you."

"She shouldn't."

"I already told her that."

I grinned. "I'm sure you were subtle."

"I prefer 'direct.'"

"Uh-huh." I clicked my tongue. "I need a favor."

"What?"

"I need you to contact Graham Porter. Tell him we need to see Seamus as soon as possible."

"Jesus Christ, Sam. Lucille calls me, I call Graham—we're your goddamned phone chain."

"I don't have a secretary."

"You can't afford a secretary."

"Not my fault I'm not rich."

"Yes it is," she said. "But I love you anyway."

People are arrogant. They think that owning a house and a small parcel of land grants them immunity from the outside world. Their home is their sanctuary, their kingdom, their holy ground. It is a place where the rules of the outside world are replaced by their own personal rules, and anyone who walks into their home is expected to immediately conform to the rules of the house.

If you think I'm making this up, ask yourself why people lock their car doors in public parking lots but feel free to leave them unlocked in their own driveway. It's just as easy for a thief to walk through your yard as it is for a thief to walk across the lot at Stop and Shop. But people in their arrogance think no one would dare disrupt their own personal sanctuary; their land means their rules.

It was this mode of thinking that allowed me to be waiting in the passenger seat of Michael Stanchion's car when he came out to go to work in the morning. The passenger seat of his Jaguar wasn't made to be comfortable to anyone over three feet tall, and I ripped a few of the staples in my side as I twisted around. A small stain appeared on my shirt from the blood. I didn't think it would be necessary, but I was sure Michael would have plenty of paper towels and cleaning supplies in the house if I started to bleed on his leather interior.

A thin sheen of frost had covered the windshield of his car, and he didn't even see me as he came out of the house. He walked to the car with the purposeful stride of a man counting off the numerous items on his itinerary for the day. Business as usual. Not bad for a man who was recently shot at in his office. Maybe I should have his friends.

He opened the door and sat down, and when he finally did notice me sitting next to him, he jumped so high he yelped as he hit his head on the roof of the car. He was wearing a camel's-hair jacket with brown slacks and a shirt and tie, but his professional attire didn't do much to hide his unease. He looked irritated, but he also looked uncomfortable. Instead of getting up and out to call the police, he slammed the door shut and turned to look at me.

"What are you doing here?" he barked.

"Healing," I said, looking straight back at him.

Stanchion's eyes lost their glare for a moment, and he looked genuinely confused. He also shut up, which marked the first time he'd done that since I met him. Seeing this as a one-time opportunity, I took the ball and ran with it.

"These are dangerous people you're dealing with, Mike."

"No kidding they're dangerous, asshole," he said.

Apparently my running game was for shit.

His voice was quiet but his arrogance had returned. "And they're probably watching me right now. They see me talking with you, and..."

"And what? They'll kill you like they killed your daughter?"

I waited. Michael stared at the steering wheel with his mouth open.

"That's it, isn't it Mike? They killed Jessica and you came to me hoping I'd kill them."

"I don't think they killed Jessica." His voice was distant. "I really don't."

"Mike, I've been offered money to leave this case. People are wandering around offering cash to have me killed. I've been stalked by a pimp from Massachusetts and jumped in a parking lot in what was obviously a planned setup. Two of them gutted me with a screwdriver." I paused. "You've got power tools in your garage. There's no telling what they'll do to you."

He turned back towards me. "I didn't know about that. Really. I hope you're not hurt too badly."

"What is going on?" I asked.

"They didn't kill Jessica." He shook his head. "It's not her. It's me. And when you started snooping around....I wasn't thinking when I hired you. And now...and with the election...I can't have your interference. I can't and they can't." He looked at me. "We need you to walk away."

"Mike, you seem to think you're on equal footing with these people. I guarantee you you're not. You are a pawn to them. An expendable pawn."

Stanchion blew air out his nose and smiled. "That's where you're wrong. They need me in that office and I want that office. And once I get in that office it will be even more equal. I have their help, but," he looked back at me, "I have a wife as well. And they are dangerous."

"I don't think you'd have a problem replacing your wife," I said, tossing him the printout picture of the blond in the campaign photo. It was a long shot, and a weak one at that, but I didn't have anything else to use at the moment.

"Talk about kicking a guy when he's down, Miller," he said, looking out the driver's side window. He crumpled up the paper. "I love my wife. Jessica's death drove that point home. This," he said, still holding the crumpled up paper, "was a mistake. It won't happen again. And if it somehow gets out to the public, I'll kill you myself. Now get out of my car. Walk away from this case. And if I see you again, it better be because you're casting a vote for me at the polls."

"Will you shake my hand if I go to a rally?" I asked as I opened the passenger-side door.

He drove off without answering.

My guess was no.

35

Last May

"How's the campaign going, Michael?"

Seamus Lynch sat back in his leather chair and raised his glass of scotch to his lips. Michael did the same. Leaned back, raised his glass, took a sip. Don't want to appear too eager. Never want to appear too eager.

"Steady," Michael replied. "Quite well, actually."

Seamus smiled and clasped his hands on his stomach.

"Do you know who I am, Michael?"

Michael hesitated.

"I know of you."

Seamus chuckled softly. "Be careful, Michael. Rumors are such ugly things. I wouldn't want you to get the wrong idea simply from things you hear around town."

He took a drink from his glass and placed it back down on his desk. Michael took a look around the room. It was pristine. Artwork on the walls, a real oak desk, leather furniture. You forgot where you were just by being here. No noise, no intrusions from the outside world. Stanchion took a swallow of his own scotch and breathed deeply through his nose. He had to play this just right.

"I'm a businessman, Michael," Seamus continued. "I like to seize opportunities as they arise; opportunities that will help enrich my life. I look at you and I see an opportunity. I see an opportunity to make my life better. More importantly, I see an opportunity to make your life better."

Lynch drained his glass and set it on the desk. Michael Stanchion did the same. This man whispered power. He whispered money. He whispered promise. Michael Stanchion liked this man very much.

"Are you interested, Michael?" Seamus Lynch asked.

"Yes," Michael answered. "I am."

"Good, Michael," Seamus said. "Good. I'm very glad. I think we're going to be able to help each other out a great deal." He leaned in close over his desk. Reflexively, Stanchion did the same. "But first, Michael, I need to know something." Stanchion nodded. He was afraid to breathe too hard, for fear he'd disturb the stillness of the room. Seamus Lynch looked straight at Michael Stanchion. "I need to know, Michael, I need to know if I can trust you."

Lil was right. I hated that about her.

I was exhausted. I'd gotten up early to meet Stanchion before he left for work and then had to walk back down the road to where I'd parked my car. By the time I got home it wasn't even ten in the morning, and I was already ready for bed.

I washed out the area where my wound had opened, made myself a sandwich, and sprawled out on the couch. There was obviously a connection between Stanchion and the mob, although I doubted it was as strong as Michael would like to believe. Graham had told Lil that Seamus would entertain a meeting with us this evening at eight. Entertain. Maybe he was hoping I'd make him laugh.

I fell asleep on the couch and woke up to the sound of Graham's Harley beneath my living room window, which was infinitely better than waking up to his face looming over me on the couch. I got up and walked through my kitchen, out the door, and down the steps to meet him in my driveway.

"Beautiful, Sammy. I'm takin' you to meet one of the premier criminal elite on the east'rn seaboard, and yer already lookin' like you was worked over twice this mornin'. Put the fear o' God inta him, ya will. Really."

"I'm as hale and hearty as a girl scout. I assume I'm driving?"

"Unless you feel like wrappin' yourself around me and holdin' on fer dear life," he said as he pulled his bike off to the side.

"Maybe later," I said, "Although I am supposed to meet Lil for a gala reception tonight at the Sandy Villa Country Club."

"Sandy Villa? Buncha snobs wit' their noses so far in the air they drown if it rains. The hell're you goin' there for?"

"Lil's brokerage is throwing some kind of party. I'm not exactly sure of the reason."

"Well then let's make sure Lynch listens politely to whatever you have to say and then get you out of there in one piece."

"I like that loyalty, my friend."

"Loyalty nothin'," he said, squeezing his 280-pound frame into my passenger side. "I just don't want Lil mad at me."

There's a lot to the man who is Graham Porter. One might take a look at him and wonder how a homeless fisherman could gain immediate access to the highest criminal echelon in the state. Like most things, there is a valid answer, and like most things, most people will never hear it.

Graham and I had bought drinks back and forth for each other one Sunday afternoon in September. We were the only patrons in the bar and were sharing our misery as we watched the Red Sox get swept, quite handily, by the Devil Rays.

You know the Devil Rays. The team from Florida that normally gets beat by everybody. Normally.

There's a camaraderie that develops between drinkers at a bar, and a camaraderie that develops between Red Sox fans as they watch their team lose, so Graham and I were already doubly friendly. The game ends and we move to the juke box, trading songs and stories that go with the songs; bands worth seeing live, songs to get laid to, and so on.

We're emptying quarters left and right into the machine. We've got blues, rock, Aerosmith, the Stones, Janis, Aretha, Buddy, Tracy, Alice—the crescendo of music is not stopping. And then Graham Porter gets up and plays the surprise of the day. He plunks in fifty cents and plays—not once, but twice—"Faithfully" by Journey. That's right; the theme song to every junior high prom from 1983 to 1987, the ballad whose opening strains rekindle memories of sweaty thirteen-year old hands and dancing resembling a capsizing boat was just requested as a double shot by a man who could arm-wrestle Sasquatch to the ground while drinking a beer.

"Well this is a change," I say.

"Fer my wife," Graham responds.

"Is she on her way over?"

"She's dead."

And then it starts.

Graham just starts talking. It's rhetoric, no emotion, just a recitation of facts, like the summation of a trial or a doctor's diagnosis. But he starts at the beginning and goes straight through to the end.

At one point in time, Graham had what would pass for a relatively normal lifestyle. He owned a fishing boat, had a wife and a little five-year-old girl, and even a modest little two-bedroom home a half mile from work. He wasn't rich, but he was happy.

That was five years ago.

Five years ago there was also a huge boom in the cocaine trade on the eastern seaboard. People were utilizing seaports up and down the coastline to pull in cocaine and then distribute it to Boston, New York, Providence, wherever there was a market for it. Seamus Lynch hadn't yet monopolized the drug trade, and Rhode Island was basically split into thirds. Providence and all points north were, for the most part, controlled by drug traffickers from Massachusetts. Erica Gold was quietly expanding her territory from Cranston down to North Kingstown, and South County was managed by a man named Ruby Vasquez.

"Managed" is really too generous a term. Vasquez was a flashy public figure who made a statement simply by wearing the loudest, brashest Hawaiian shirts that could be found and sporting three gold chains on what some would describe as chest hair but actually resembled chicken wire more than anything else. He slicked his hair back with a Grecian formula that made him look like he was constantly perspiring, drove a hot pink Falcon convertible around town, and carried a thermos with him that was filled with Popov vodka so he could make himself a martini at any given hour of the day. Obviously a real winner, but what do you expect from a guy named Ruby?

I never even met the man; I just heard the description from Graham. But c'mon, even if Graham was given to exaggeration, which he's not, who the hell could make that up? Ruby had established himself as the drug kingpin of South County, which basically meant that Ruby had loudly announced that if anyone wanted drugs, come to him and he would take care of you. It was a very poorly kept secret; in fact it wasn't even a secret at all, but as Lucille had discussed earlier, Ruby also distanced himself so far from the actual product that the police were hung up with the problem of trying to find some way to tie him to the drugs, and as such, Narragansett was left with a very flamboyant version of Al Capone.

Ruby was never that bright a bulb, but watching the police get their hands tied when trying to deal with him also bolstered his arrogance, a quality that not only grew at a rapid pace, but also spread quickly through his family tree. One relative in particular, Ruby's nephew, Dino Kitch, reveled in the living legacy his uncle was rapidly passing to him. At age fifteen, Dino was making runs for Ruby, at seventeen he was handling the cash accounts, and at nineteen he was directing the actual imports.

For a nineteen-year-old, he was loving life. And why shouldn't he? He had the world by the balls: money, girls, notoriety, and power. Christ, he was Tommy Bates on a statewide scale. But he was still nineteen. And where normal nineteen-year-olds have a certain feeling of invulnerability, Dino's arrogance had been cultivated to become his driving force. He only had two questions when he woke up in the morning: What do I want and how do I get it? He had never had reason to think anything else.

So the cocaine shipments have been coming in a little at a time, making their way inwards from the east, keeping everyone happy, but Dino wants more. He's not satisfied with the small consistent shipments coming in bits at a time. Like any kid he wants bigger, faster, better. We're not getting caught moving small shipments in on the boats, Dino thinks. If it's working for the small shipments, it should work for a big shipment. If people can't tell we're moving it now, they can't tell we're moving it at all. No need to be chickenshit, he thinks. We increase our product, we increase our cash.

So Dino and three friends he has allowed to become employed as bodyguards stroll up and down the docks looking for the right boat for his great idea. They come across Graham and his boat, the *Lady Maria*, which Graham has named after his wife. They look at Graham's hulking body, his muscles stretched across his body like cables as he hauls crates off his boat, and they think, shit, this motherfucker's not gonna be afraid of anything.

They saunter up to the end of the pier and wait for Graham to notice them. Graham, of course, had noticed them the instant they got out of their car. How could you not? Teenagers dressed in silk shirts and pressed pants; sporting more necklaces, bracelets, rings, and earrings between the four of them than most women wear, but Dino always demands that his crew looks their best.

Graham's wife has one pair of earrings. Diamonds. Small. Graham had to work three years before he could afford them.

The kids take off their sunglasses and put them in their shirt pockets and smile and wait for this bear of a man to come over and help them get rich. Graham ignores them and continues to unload his boat, so they walk over to him, hands outstretched, Dino introducing everyone. It's a wasted effort—Graham knows who they are. Dino shares his uncle's same taste for public fame and recognition.

Dino pulls a brick of cocaine wrapped in aluminum foil out of a bag and hands it to Graham. Then he pulls out a wrap of hundred dollar bills and places it in Graham's other hand. He tells Graham that's what he'll give him for each crate he fills with coke and then carries into port on his boat.

Now, like I said, Graham associates with some less-than-savory people, and he's not above breaking a few laws now and then if it suits his purpose. He looks at the stack of bills in his right hand, and it's not even his wife Maria he thinks of, but his daughter Annabeth. Graham's not a rich man. This cash could make sure his daughter has the things she needs growing up. She'd be taken care of.

Graham looks at the brick in his left hand. He's seen people on coke. He looks at Dino and his friends. He knows what they do in his town. He doesn't want his daughter to have to deal with that side of life as she grows up. He won't be party to helping that element grow and flourish in her town.

Graham says no and hands the stack of bills back to Dino. Dino slaps another stack on top. One for each crate he says. The more you carry, the more you make. Capitalism at its best, man.

Graham says no again, giving the money back a little more forcefully and pushing Dino in the chest as he does so. Dino's boys tense; they know their role, but pushing back on this titanic of a man doesn't seem too smart. They stand their ground, nervously, and watch as Dino is rebuked again.

Dino loses it. Who the fuck is this guy? Tell me no? Shove me? Trouble is, Graham can shove Dino all he wants, and there's not much Dino can do about it. But remember, Dino's a kid, and arrogant as hell, and he gets in Graham's face and just starts screaming. Do you know who I am? Do you know what I can do?

Graham doesn't give a fuck who this kid is. And no way in hell is he going to waste his time in a screaming match with a little snot-nosed punk like this. But again, he thinks of his little girl Annabeth. He doesn't want her to have to deal with this type of shit as she grows up. Graham turns around and walks back onto his boat. He's still carrying the brick of cocaine in his hand. Dino's screaming has attracted the attention of anyone in the vicinity, and everyone has stopped what they're doing and diverted their attention to him. Graham leans over the side of his boat, rips open the package of cocaine, and dumps the contents into the water. Then he turns to Dino and tells him if he ever tries to carry his shit onto the docks again, he, Graham Porter, will personally break his legs.

Dino stares at Graham, and then he and his adolescent posse get back in Dino's car and drive away. He drives to his Uncle Ruby's house where he finds his uncle sitting in his living room in a bright yellow Hawaiian shirt drinking a Popov martini. He tells his uncle how he was just publicly humiliated by this fisherman in front of a crowd of people.

Ruby's cocky, Ruby's cocked, and Ruby's in one of his let-me-tell-you-the-ways-of-the-world moods. He explains to Dino that all you have in this world is your reputation. Your reputation can make you or break you, and this man on the docks has just brought your rep down a couple of notches. You need to get your rep back up to the top.

Dino nods after Ruby's done talking. Ruby is very wise. He's a sage. He's the man. Of course he's the man. Didn't he give Dino a Rolex watch for his birthday, complete with the inscription, *Dino, Happy 18th, Uncle Ruby*? Ruby knows what he's talking about. He's shown him the way. Again.

Dino doesn't even ask what's the best way to reclaim his rep, because Dino already has his mind made up: You fuck with me; I fuck with you. Schoolyard rules, and Dino is literally just three months out of the schoolyard.

Dino is also hopped up on his own product more often than not and gets his idea while he is enjoying a particularly strong buzz. It's crystal clear. It makes perfect sense. And best of all, it will teach Graham and the community that you can't fuck with Dino Kitch.

Dino gets his squad together, and they smoke a gloriously potent rock while he explains his plan. It will take some work, but the four of them can pull it off. It will take some time, but the sooner they get started, the sooner they'll be done.

The hardest part is getting Graham. They shoot him with a tranquilizer, and it sounds corny, but they had to shoot him twice before he goes down. The four of them tie him up and load him into the back of the stolen pickup truck Dino's friend Howard found. Even with four of them they had trouble lifting him up, but they do it.

Dino would like to think that slapping Graham in the face is what brought him around, but the truth of it was that the tranquilizer wears off much quicker than expected. Regardless, Graham awakes to find himself covered by a heavy tarp, his hands and legs tied in rope, and a heavy chain wrapped around his waist. Graham may be a bear of a man, but even he wasn't going anywhere right now.

He looks around to get his surroundings and slowly realizes he's sitting in his living room, his own living room in his own house. He tries to move and realizes that the chain wrapped around him is secured to the chair on which he's sitting. Dino is screaming something in his left ear, but Graham doesn't hear what he was saying. He is trapped into looking in front of him. In front of him is his wife, Maria, stripped naked, and his daughter, Annabeth, five years old, also stripped naked.

There's no doubt in Graham's mind what is about to happen. If his muscles would respond, they still wouldn't be able to free him from his trappings, but however futile, at least it would allow him to think he was making an effort to save his family. Instead, he's forced to sit still and watch.

Dino's friends take turns violating Maria in every way possible. In front, in back, on top, orally, anally, laughing like a couple of teenagers the whole time. They are a couple of teenagers. Maria keeps a blank stare focused on nothing as they swarm over her. Every so often she steals a glance over at her daughter, sitting on Howard's lap, watching her mother in quiet concern.

Graham watches in silence and remembers every detail.

Dino continues to whisper in Graham's ear as they finish with Maria. Howard then unzips his pants and places Annabeth, five-year-old Annabeth, on top of him and starts to plunge himself into her over and over. Annabeth starts to cry, which makes Howard plunge in harder. Maria screams for them to stop, but Dino's friends hold her down.

Graham watches in silence and remembers every detail.

Annabeth's cries get louder, Maria continues to scream, and Dino starts waving his gun around yelling at everyone to shut up. Howard had smoked more of the rock than anybody and is laughing with glee as he slams himself into Annabeth over and over, but her crying is really starting to annoy the shit out of him. He climaxes inside of her; he's done with her, but the bitch just won't shut up.

So Howard takes her head in his hands and twists, breaking her neck.

"Help me, Daddy," was the last thing she said.

Maria loses it. She bites, she claws, she kicks, she screams. Dino's boys let her go, but before she can run to her baby, Dino fires his gun five times, and Maria is nothing more than a bloody, faceless, lifeless slab of meat on the floor.

Graham watches everything in silence and remembers every detail.

Dino leans in and whispers one more time to Graham. Tells him you don't mess with Dino Kitch. You don't play Dino Kitch for a fool. Tells him Dino Kitch has the biggest dick on the block.

They pump him up with sedatives one more time and load him back into the truck. Then they set fire to his house and let it burn to the ground.

Graham is dumped back on his boat and Dino and his boys drove away. They'd accomplished what they'd set out to do: break Graham and set an example for the rest of the community.

Word traveled very quickly. Again, Dino was very arrogant. And very young. He needed to sate his ego. He wanted people to know what he had done;

he wanted people to know he was in charge; and he wanted people to know they should be afraid of him. And they were. But they were also disgusted.

Dino was very loud. And like I said, there is nothing that passes through the docks that Graham doesn't hear or see.

The *Lady Maria* made a couple of unscheduled runs over the next week.

Over the next week a few grotesque discoveries were made as well.

The *Liberty* reined in a pair of human hands and one foot with its fishing nets. A headless corpse washed up on the children's beach down the road. The *Walking Sunset*'s anchor dragged up a human body minus the head, feet, and one arm.

The fish had already started feeding on this one.

The police worked to identify the bodies off of swollen fingerprints and came to the conclusion that the corpses were the three friends of Dino. Of course the police questioned Graham, but it seemed everybody in the world had seen Graham drinking in the local taverns over the last week, and three women came forward to state they had stayed the night with him at one time or another to help him through his misery.

That was good enough for the police. They didn't press Graham any harder. Dino had been very loud. Everyone knew what he'd done to Graham's family. Losing filth like this could only improve the town. In a different time they would've given Graham a medal. They didn't even book the prostitutes who stated they had spent the night with him.

No one ever saw or heard from Dino Kitch again. But Ruby Vasquez received a package in the mail shortly thereafter containing two eyes, a handful of teeth, and Dino's Rolex watch, complete with inscription.

All the Popov in the world couldn't keep Ruby from understanding what that meant. He packed up his Hawaiian shirts and got the hell out of Dodge. He left a lot of coked-up addicts in the lurch by doing that, and millions of untapped dollars behind. But Ruby was scared, and rightly so. His nephew had been correct in his initial assessment of Graham: This motherfucker's not afraid of anything.

Things quieted down a bit after that; Graham insured that happened. Seamus Lynch started growing roots in Providence, and Erica Gold puttered around in South County, but kept to herself. Nothing came in or off the boats.

Eventually Seamus took over the majority of the state. The boats were unused, and as far as he was concerned, that was a waste. He sent four of his men down to deal with Graham. Graham sent one of them back alive.

Seamus wasn't stupid, and neither was Graham. Eventually Seamus would get what he wanted; Graham was, after all, only one man. The question was how many men was Lynch willing to lose in the process? Seamus came down to visit with Graham himself. Actually had a sit-down meeting with him; Lynch in a three-piece suit and wingtips, Graham in work boots and jeans, his T-shirt barely containing the muscles of his body. Shared a drink in the fuckin' Rusty Nail and came to agreement on business terms in one of the more bizarre power lunches in the history of free enterprise.

Seamus walked out of the tavern with the ability to use South County as a base of operations. There were plenty of restaurants through which he could launder his money and deal with clientele.

But Galilee was off-limits.

Working the boats was the sole source of income for the majority of people on the docks. Graham didn't want to see that taken away or fucked up in any manner. Lynch was free to come around and hire muscle if he needed it. Graham himself worked for him when the opportunity presented itself. But the boats themselves were prohibited. Graham got what he wanted, Lynch got what he wanted, and a respectful balance was struck. That balance was what was getting me a front-row seat with Seamus Lynch now.

Graham Porter was a very hard-working man. In his own right he was a businessman; time was not wasted and nothing was done for free. Fish were caught and sold. If Lynch needed someone threatened, Porter got paid. Everything had a price and nothing was done out of the "goodness of your heart." No such thing as a favor.

Graham had told me his help was "on the house." He didn't do that for anybody. I knew that, and he knew I knew that.

It gave me a good feeling.

The bar was named Rudder's. It was located on the southernmost tip of Point Judith. At first glance it appeared to be a good old-fashioned dive, and upon closer inspection it was revealed that this was indeed the case. The outside of the bar resembled an almost quaint cottage home with placard siding and weather-beaten shingles, but the interior barely made it look like a basement.

The first floor housed a large square bar that took up maybe half the room. At the front half of the room a band was setting up, but there was no stage, just the flat concrete floor. Three tables were lined up against the far wall, but other than that, it looked like Rudder's catered to a standing-room-only crowd. At eight o'clock on a Tuesday evening there wasn't much of a crowd for us to maneuver through.

The bartender looked up as Graham and I walked through the door, and almost immediately a man with deeply gelled and styled blond hair appeared from out of nowhere. He was wearing a white button-down shirt under a blue sweater-vest and freshly pressed khakis, and he smelled of expensive cologne. He greeted Graham and then turned to walk with us, escorting us through the nonexistent crowd.

We walked through a doorway in the back corner that opened into a stairwell and up a flight of stairs. The second floor housed a small kitchen and wraparound deck where patrons could sit outside and eat and watch seagulls fly away with half of their food. We climbed to the third floor and stopped outside the door at the top of the stairs. The J. Crew model who had walked us thus far turned to face us.

"Please divulge any weapons, gentlemen," he said, extending his arms with his palms up.

I took my gun off my hip and gave it to J. Crew. He put it in his pants pocket. Graham handed over two guns, a Bowie hunting knife, and a three-foot-long piece of chain.

"No brass knuckles?" I asked.

Graham gave a faint smile.

Our escort seemed momentarily at a loss as to what to do with Graham's collection and settled for storing everything in a small pile in the corner. He then turned back to us and twirled his hands in little circles.

"If you please, gentlemen."

Graham and I both spread our legs and leaned forward, placing our palms against the wall. We were quickly but thoroughly patted down and, upon passing inspection, straightened ourselves back up.

"Please be advised, Mr. Porter," the gentleman said with his hand on the doorknob, "Mr. Lynch is not one who has time to spend on frivolous matters. He is granting this meeting out of respect to you, but should he become agitated..." He let the sentence trail off.

"I'll try not t'piss on the rug if he makes me nervous," Graham said and moved a step closer. The landing at the top of the stairway was small, and the gentleman had no choice but to turn the knob and open the door. Two more steps and we followed him inside.

If the devil wore a business suit, he would've looked like Seamus Lynch.

He sat behind a desk that made Stanchion's look like it was picked up at a yard sale. He wore an olive pin-striped suit, buttoned at the waist over a blue silk shirt and matching tie. His cufflinks and tie tack glimmered in the sunset from the window behind him. His silver hair was neatly styled back, and even his eyebrows arched in a freshly blow-dried manner. He wore no jewelry, and his hands rested calmly on the desktop in front of him. If not for the obviously healthy color that resonated from him, I would've fully expected a gold-topped walking stick to be resting against his desk.

A rich, burgundy-colored rug covered the office floor, and once our escort closed the door, any trace of the bar below us was shut out. Lynch motioned to two chairs in front of his desk, and Graham and I walked noiselessly across the carpet and sat in them. J. Crew stood behind Lynch with his hands clasped languidly in front of him. Seated in the corner behind Lynch's desk was Corey Runter. He was immaculately attired, as I suspected he always was. He still wore his trench coat and let it unfold around him on the chair. He crossed his legs, leaned back in his chair, and rested his hands on his stomach. As we sat down he winked at me, and a smile seemed to float off his face and evaporate in the air. We all sat looking at each other for a moment in silence. Finally Seamus Lynch straightened up in his chair and cleared his throat.

"Mr. Miller," he began, "While I must admit it is impressive to see you sitting here before me, it is not, in any way, shape, or form, pleasurable."

"You'd be amazed how many people greet me the same way," I smiled.

"And I have to wonder," he continued, "why it is that the political campaign of a local resident is of such concern to a petty, two-bit hustler such as yourself."

"We have so much in common, Seamus. That's the exact question I was going to ask you."

Lynch's eyes flashed for a moment before they settled back to their cold blue. To the right of me, Graham chuckled.

"Get to the point, Mr. Miller. Before I remember how truly inconsequential you are and have Charles here throw you out."

"Well let's start there then," I said. "Explain to me how you can be running this vast criminal empire and employing people like dick-in-his-mouth Charlie here. Chrissake, Seamus, he's gonna be too worried about messing up his hair to push me down the stairs."

"Hey—" Charles started.

"And Runter is nothing more than a guy who's seen *The Godfather* one too many times. He can't even have me killed in a supermarket."

Runter was standing directly behind Lynch, his gun drawn and pointed at me over Lynch's left shoulder. His trench coat remained draped across his chair. I never even saw him move.

"Wouldn't be a problem now," he grinned.

Graham blew out a burst of breath, as if he were bored, and stood up. Corey, even though he had his gun out and the desk between him and Graham, took a step back involuntarily. Charles looked around and tried not to wet himself.

"Enough," Seamus glared, trying, and failing, to hide his aggravation.

"I don't get it," I said. "You don't seem that dumb, Seamus. Then again, I've been wrong before. Personally, I think Stanchion's a moron. He seems to think he can go toe to toe with you. I hear he's great in the courtroom, but…I dunno. I can't guess what you want with Michael Stanchion. But don't you worry. I'll figure it out."

Corey smirked at me from in back of Lynch. I smiled graciously at Lynch. Lynch gave me a hard stare. One big happy family. Lynch continued giving me his glare a moment longer, then turned his attention to Graham.

"If you and your friend are finished," he said, his voice contained, "please show yourself out."

Graham had returned to his seat, looking like a high school student wondering when the hell the bell would ring so he could get on with his life. I wondered if he gave lessons to Tommy Bates. He turned his head in my direction. "You all set?" he asked.

"Sure."

He shrugged. "OK." He got up out of his chair. J. Crew took a full step back, although I don't think he realized it. Graham extended his hand. "Thanks for the time." Seamus shook it and nodded. Graham looked at me and motioned towards the door. I got up and held out my hand to J. Crew, who handed me back my gun. Graham followed me to the door. I opened it, and Graham took his time collecting his weapons, which were still in a pile at the top of the stairs. He turned around and, holding his hunting knife in his hand, pointed at Seamus Lynch.

"Thanks again," he said. Then he turned and we both started down the stairwell.

J. Crew didn't follow us down.

"So did we accomplish anything here?" I asked as we went back down the stairs.

"Yeah. You irritated the snot outta Seamus Lynch."

"Ah."

"Was there anytin' in particula' that you wanted to accomplish?"

"I was kinda hoping to irritate the snot out of Seamus Lynch."

"Ah."

We reached the ground floor. Graham looked at me. "Mission accomplished."

He opened the door and we walked back into the bar on the first floor. The patrons had increased, not substantially, but enough so you could probably call it a crowd. Two of the band members were still setting up, while other members had moved on to talking with the ladies who were using their speakers as bar stools. Graham and I walked up to the bar and sat down.

I ordered a gin and tonic for myself and a beer for Graham. The bartender brought them over.

"These are on the house, Mr. Porter," the bartender said.

I raised my glass. "I should hang out with you more often," I said.

"Ruin my image." He took a swallow of his beer. "Y'know Sammy, if all you wanted t'do was insult Lynch, ya could've just sent him a postcard. Why'd ya want this meetin' shit?"

"Man needs to know I'm not scared."

Graham swiveled on his stool so he was looking at me. "Yeah, he does," he nodded, and clinked my glass with his mug. "Now let's just make sure he doesn't need you dead."

"That'd be nice."

I took a sip of my drink and looked out into the crowd. Most of it was made up of college kids out of classes for the day, looking to blow off some steam or find someone to go home with, or maybe both. The attire of choice was blue jeans and some sort of top designed to either show off your cleavage or accentuate your biceps; either way would get you noticed. The other way to be guaranteed to be noticed was to be the only patron in the bar wearing a three-piece suit, which, while slumped in a seat at a corner table nursing his drink, was exactly what Michael Stanchion was doing.

I nudged Graham with my elbow. "You see what I see?"

Graham looked over at Stanchion.

"Golly gosh."

"Golly gosh?"

"Holy fuck."

I nodded. "Holy fuck."

It wasn't just his attire that made Stanchion seem out of place. He hunched over his drink and cast furtive glances around the bar. Gone was the patronizing, arrogant master of men who had told me what to do every other time I'd met him. In his place sat a plump, balding man hiding in the corner, ill at ease with his surroundings, hoping to be noticed without being seen.

"Looks a little nervous," Graham observed.

"That he does," I said. "Think we oughta go over and make him feel more comfortable?"

"Oh yeah," Graham chuckled. "We just the two t'do dat."

Graham set his beer mug down and pushed himself off his stool. Ignoring decades of practice and discipline, I left a half-finished drink on the bar and followed him over.

"Good evening," I said, taking a seat across the table from Stanchion. Graham pulled out the seat next to Michael and sat down. If Stanchion was trying to hide in a crowd, Graham was now basically blocking him off from view of everyone in the bar. He looked up as we sat down with him and then looked quickly back down at the table, as if not looking at us meant we weren't really there.

"What are you doing here?" he asked.

I signaled for the waitress to come over and ordered a round of drinks. "Put it on his tab," I said, gesturing at Stanchion. He continued to look at the table.

"Been upstairs shooting the breeze with your bosses, Seamus and Corey," I said. "'Course, soon as we mention your name, they throw us out. Can't exactly figure out why. You wanna help us out on this?"

Michael met my eyes for the first time. "Corey Runter's here?"

"Mm-hmm," I nodded.

He looked around. "You've got to get me out of here."

"Why?"

"Why?! He wants to kill me! For chrissake, Miller, it was Runter who shot at me in my office!"

"Yeah, shot at me too."

"Don't put yerself first," Graham murmured. "Rude."

"Did you hear me?" Stanchion was doing his best not to shout. "Corey Runter wants to kill me!"

I looked at Graham.

"What a senseless travesty dat would be," he said.

"Senseless."

"Tragic."

"Can one say 'travist'?"

"Never heard nobody use dat word."

"Well if one can take 'tragedy' and get 'tragic,' what can one get from 'travesty'?"

"One of the eternal mysteries of life, dat would be dere."

Michael Stanchion pulled the sleeve of my jacket. "Shut up," he pleaded. "Please! If Runter is here, you have to get me out of here. Now!!"

Always good to have your nonpaying client who's fired you asking you to risk your life to protect him. Portfolio builder.

"Be a pleasure," I said.

The three of us stood up. I nodded towards the front door, and Graham took a light grip on Stanchion's arm and led the way through the crowd. As we passed the band two men fell into step beside us, one of whom I recognized from the other afternoon at the Royal Arms hotel. We all filed out the front door and into the parking lot. The parking lot wasn't much more than a couple hundred square feet of tightly packed sand, and the rain had started up steadily again, creating pockets of puddles all around us. Behind us we heard the band begin to play. Two more men appeared to our left, so we were now more or less surrounded by the four. I looked at Graham. We both knew where this was heading, and there was nothing to do now but ride it out.

"This way, if you please, gentlemen," one of them said, leading us around the side of the building.

Normally I would have just said "no" but Stanchion had already started marching around the corner, and I wasn't about to lose him this time. Of course, his eager acquiescence could quite easily lead to my death, but I'm not sure that concerned him. Lucky me.

We walked behind the bar and down a slight hill. The ground began to sink beneath our footsteps as we reached a small marsh, and waist-high weeds climbed up all around us. Behind us we heard the band in full swing.

"Not the most engaging place to die," I heard Corey Runter's voice say from within the darkness. "But it will have to do."

I had to wonder if he wrote his own dialogue or hired someone to feed it to him. He stepped out of the marsh into the small area made visible by the outside lights on the bar behind us. The belt of his trench coat was fastened tightly around his waist, a fedora covered his head, and his collar was pulled tight around his neck. His hands were encased firmly in his pockets. The rain bore down harder.

"Shoot them," he barked. "All three of them."

My gut clenched. Nobody moved.

Runter looked from side to side. "I said shoot!"

"I—I dunno, Mr. Runter," one of the men started. "Mr. Lynch said we was just supposed to bring Mr. Stanchion back inside. He didn't say nothing about shooting. Especially with Mr. Porter here—"

"I don't care what Lynch said." A burst of light exploded from his trench coat pocket. The man Runter shot staggered backward. Corey finished pulling his gun out and fired twice more into his chest. The man's blood mixed in with the mud as he fell back into the weeds and lay still.

I knocked Stanchion down and pushed him down the hill. Graham tackled two of the remaining men like a linebacker. The third man ran back up the hill. Back in the bar we heard the band start playing "Mustang Sally." God, I hate that song. Runter kept firing. In my direction, of course.

I moved through the weeds on my stomach, trying to circle around in back of Runter. I didn't get that far, but he stopped to reload, and beggars can't be choosers. I was on the left side of him and sprinted up towards him. My feet kept slipping in the dirt, and I half fell, half dove into his waist. It didn't knock him all the way down, but it jarred the gun out of his hand momentarily.

Runter kicked me in the face and I went down. I started to get up, and he kicked me again. I spit up some blood. The lights on the bar looked much brighter than they should have.

"I should have killed the two of you the first time," I heard him say.

I knew he was reaching for his gun. I told my body to get up, but it was responding about six speeds too slow. I also knew Graham was coming up the hill. I couldn't see him, but when he runs, he makes less noise than a rhinoceros. I heard a sound best described as "hrrrkkk," and when I finally got to my knees, Corey Runter's body was lying face down in front of me, and Graham was to my right, wiping the blade of his knife on the weeds.

"You all right?" he asked, looking at me.

"Yep," I nodded, getting my breathing back.

"He had a line on you. Hadda go down."

"This one still on the house?"

"I'll send you a bill." He reached over and picked the fedora off the back of Runter's head. "Always wanted a fedora. Bet it makes me look like Indiana Jones."

He put the hat on and stood up. I got to my feet and looked down into the marsh.

"Think Stanchion's still here?"

"He's long gone, buddy." Graham looked over at the two men he had knocked down. One was sitting up, the other was still inert. "We all done here?" he called down. "Or we still fightin'?"

"We never meant to go after you, Mr. Porter," he called back. "That was all Mr. Runter. We're very sorry."

"No harm, no foul," he said. "Tell your boss he's got some cleanup out here."

Graham paused to light a cigarette in the rain, and then we turned and started walking up the hill.

"Rhode Island just lost a pimp," he said.

"S'okay. I'll see if Lil will unionize the hookers."

We walked across the dirt parking lot to the Mustang. Inside the bar, the band was playing "Sweet Home Alabama." Graham looked at me over the roof of the car.

"Your eye's startin' to swell."

"I'm a swell guy."

"Sure are," he laughed.

We got in the car and drove out of the parking lot.

No one shot at us as we left.

"Strike you funny that Stanchion didn't stick aroun' to see if we wuz OK, or thank us for savin' his ass?" Graham asked as we drove home.

"Maybe he ran straight to the police," I said. "Could be there right now giving an in-depth statement."

"Sure."

"Strikes me funny that we found him in Lynch's bar in the first place."

"And it also comical that Runter seemed very intent on shootin' him."

"After he shot at me."

"Always have t'put yerself first. Insecure ego." Graham adjusted his fedora and leaned back in his seat. "While we in the midst o' bein' struck funny by all dis, p'rhaps we might notice some sorta connection."

"You mean like a clue?"

"You the professional."

"I've heard rumors."

I pulled into my driveway. Graham got out. So did I.

"You gonna lose the fedora while you're on the bike?"

"I'll drive slow."

I walked him to his Harley.

"Thank you," I said, extending my hand. Graham's paw swallowed a quarter of my arm as he shook it. I wondered if I would ever see my hand again.

"My pleasure," he said. "My regards t'Lil."

"You'll be scoring points when I tell her what a snappy dresser you're becoming."

Graham fired up his motorcycle.

"I score any more points," he said, "An' I'll be higher'n you."

He gunned the motor and drove off. I heard his engine echo down the road. As far as I could tell, the fedora stayed on.

The motor in the Mustang was still running. I got back inside and sat down. I leaned back in the seat and let the hot air blow over me. The clock on the dash read nine twenty. It would take at least fifteen minutes to drive to Lil's party, and that was due to end at ten. I closed my eyes and laughed. In the last hour I had threatened a minor crime lord, been shot at, and been witness to two deaths caused basically because I had ordered and demanded a meeting with Seamus Lynch, and here I was worried because I'd be late for a date.

I laughed again, but this time it caught in my throat and ended as a wheezing cough. I felt my side and it was wet with blood. My staples had ripped open. I looked at myself in the mirror. My face was covered in dirt, and I'd be lucky if nothing tried to nest in my hair. The rest of my body was a winning mixture of salt marsh and blood. I was not exactly Prince Charming; but a promise is a promise.

Sandy Villa Country Club was one of the locations in Narragansett that allowed certain residents to be assured they were indeed wealthy and others in the community to sit up and take notice of that fact. Translated, that meant it was a banquet hall and golf course that was overly plush, overpriced, and, I'm sure, overrated. I made it to the grounds in ten minutes, but the final half mile from the gate to the banquet hall took almost just as long.

I got inside the gates fine, but I had to give everything short of a blood sample to the security guard to prove that I was indeed on the guest list. Once he reluctantly agreed, I pulled down the driveway to the curb of the banquet facility, gave my keys to the valet, and limped up the steps and in the front entrance.

The hallway outside the ballroom was small but stylish, and I caught my reflection in the full-length mirror standing opposite the washrooms. Taking in the blood-soaked entire left side of my shirt and long gash in my jeans, I applauded myself for making it this far inside. Realizing that even the caterers were dressed better than me, I gave a quick prayer of thanks that it was quarter of ten and walked in.

Had the DJ been playing records instead of CDs, you most certainly would have heard the screech of the needle being pulled off the LP. As it was, I could brag that my entrance ended every individual conversation in such a synchronized method that time and sound seemed to actually stop for a moment. Until, of course, a large woman who resembled a bull elephant in a pink business suit marched heavily towards me.

"What in the world are you doing here?" she said. "Harold, attend to this immediately, please. I'm paying your salary to host a premier event; not to run a homeless shelter or a soup kitchen!" Her eyes remained focused in amazement on me, but when she snapped her fingers, three men to her left jumped to attention. "Have this man removed!!"

"Relax, Carol. He's here by invitation."

I heard Lil's voice before I saw her, but once again time seemed to freeze as she walked to the front of the room. She was dressed simply in a full-length black dress and seemed to glide across the ballroom. She walked down two steps and stood next to Carol, whose hair seemed to have gotten progressively grayer in the last three minutes. That was not, I daresay, an improvement.

"I beg your pardon?" Carol said as Lil smiled at me.

"He's with me."

Lil walked over and gave me a kiss on my right cheek, which was probably the only clean spot on my entire body.

"You shaved."

"You noticed." I paused. "I didn't bring you any flowers."

"I don't know why. You look like you've made a thorough search of your neighbor's front lawn."

"He didn't have any roses."

Lil smiled again, which brightened the entire first floor of the banquet hall.

"You're just in time," she said, taking my hand. "It's the last dance."

Carol cleared her throat. "Really Lillian," she said. "You are a lovely girl. You represent an outstanding firm. But, darling, we need to raise your taste in companions to a higher quality. I mean, come now, Lillian, this *is* the Sandy Villa."

Lil turned and gave her full attention to her boss for the first time.

"Suck my left tit, Carol."

The crowd parted as we made our way to the dance floor.

You really, really, really had to love this girl.

I awoke the next morning in the same shape in which I had gone to bed: I was still breathing and I hurt like hell. There was a note next to the bed from Lil saying she had errands to run, and she'd call me sometime over the next few days. The note was under a bottle of aspirin, which was as close as Lil got to playing Florence Nightingale.

I got up and took two aspirin with a glass of orange juice. I stood in my living room and looked out my sliding-glass door at the beach. The water was calm. The sky wasn't cloudy, but was a grey color that heralded cold weather. A lone car drove along the street. The quiet was nice.

Graham was right. Something had been brewing between Lynch and Stanchion and Runter. If we figured out the connection, we'd have a big piece of the puzzle and be that much closer to finding out why Jessica Stanchion had to die on a beach in Newport before she even graduated high school.

I needed to think. I put the Stones' *Some Girls* album in the Mustang and pulled out of my driveway. There wasn't a bad song on the album, and that gave me one less thing to have to worry about.

Lynch ran drugs. Runter ran prostitution. Stanchion ran for office. There was no way if elected Mike was going to be able to legalize drugs and prostitution.

Could he turn a blind eye? Absolutely. Could he get a cut of the profits? Probably already was. He wasn't getting shot at by Runter because Corey was a Democrat. That still didn't explain why Stanchion's daughter was in the ground with two bullets in her.

I was driving up Route 108. The traffic was moderate as normal people went to normal jobs. For a brief moment I entertained the notion of becoming a truck driver and receiving a steady paycheck for the rest of my life. I stopped at a red light behind a Lexus with the license plate "LUTHER." I was pretty sure I could guess the name of the driver of the car. Twenty bucks said the truck driver behind me could too. And he was getting paid today.

Stanchion's son dealt drugs. Heroin, by his own admission. Was in jail for it as a matter of fact. Wouldn't be hard to pop him in prison. Be downright easy as a matter of fact. And he was serving time already. No reason to knock off his sister. Stanchion's daughter however...he himself had said, "I don't think they killed Jessica." The thought had crossed his mind. He'd defended Runter in court, yet Runter was the one shooting at him. It didn't make sense.

I stopped at the Mobil station and picked up a newspaper. I turned down Ocean Road and parked along the sea wall to read it. Tommy Bates had twelve rebounds and three fouls in last night's game, Hagar the Horrible was plundering a castle, and Dagwood knocked over the mailman on his way to work. Other than that, there really wasn't anything noteworthy to report.

I drove along the water and into the north end of town and turned down the street to Stanchion's house. His driveway was empty. I stopped while two joggers crossed the street, and then headed back up the main road. I passed a guy in a black truck with a dog in the back on its haunches, perched over the cab watching the world go by.

I was very jealous of that dog.

I took the long way home, driving along the water. The people out walking were sparse; most were at work or in school. The opening shifts of some of the restaurants arrived at work, sweeping off the steps and setting the tables in hopes of a lunch crowd. The sun blazed overhead, streaming through my windshield, erasing any knowledge of the forty-degree weather outside the car.

I looped down the other end of town and drove by Rudder's. It was quiet. No cars in the parking lot. No police tape sectioning off the back lot. And I was pretty sure there would be no blood traces left down by the marsh. The police weren't going to complain if Corey Runter stopped showing his face in town, and Seamus Lynch wasn't about to invite the police down to his establishment to report two shootings.

I left the parking lot and drove home. By the time I walked into my kitchen, the sun was a blinding high noon and I had made it through the Stones' album almost twice. I didn't know where the hell Michael Stanchion was, I didn't have a clue who killed his daughter, and in truth, the only concrete fact my morning drive had confirmed was that Charlie Watts was one of the most phenomenal drummers on the planet.

But I already knew that.

42

Last May

Fuckable.

If there was indeed such a word (and by all accounts Tommy believed that there should be) that would be the perfect word to describe Gloria Hurdtz.

Fuckable, fuck-happy, fuck-a-licious, whatever. The woman loved sex. They never even made it to the pizza place that first night. She did him in the parking lot. In her car. Since then, they'd done it in a supply closet, in the locker room, in her office, and at her place. She wasn't big on conversation; there was never dinner. It was simply wham-bam-wham-bam-wham-bam-thank-you-ma'am.

Fine by Tommy. Made things less complicated. Besides, he still liked Jessica. Jessica was pretty, she was smart, and she was realistic. But Ms. Hurdtz, c'mon—take it while it's there. Jessica wasn't letting him get anywhere, that was certain.

Jessica had her rules, her parents, her principles. The Winter Dance had been a bust. She looked great, she smelled great, but the buck stopped there. No way he was getting her out of her ballroom dress. No way at all. Parents probably had a fuckin' alarm built in it anyway.

Jessica was pretty, she was sweet, and yeah, Tommy had to admit she was actually a lot of fun. He liked her. But if Ms. Hurdtz wanted to throw him a treat every so often, he wasn't gonna decline.

She made him promise to keep it a secret. If anybody found out, there'd be real trouble, she said. Tommy never came right out and told anyone about it. But he hinted. Of course he hinted. People drew the right conclusions. He was a living legend in the school. Why shouldn't he be scoring Gloria Hurdtz?

And he was pretty sure a part of her wanted people to know too. She liked attention. She liked to feel wanted. Desired. And pretty. Yeah, a part of her was screaming to let people know, too.

It was a game. Tommy loved games. He'd stroll through the library and pull Jessica in close to him while he walked past Gloria. Put his arm around Jessica, smile at her, give her a quick kiss, all the while knowing Ms. Hurdtz was watching and hating every minute of it.

Jealous. It was ridiculous, really. A grown woman jealous of a teenage girl. It made Tommy laugh out loud. He remembered one time he looked up to see Ms. Hurdtz over at her desk, staring at Jessica with a look of insurmountable hatred. Insurmountable. Gloria Hurdtz was mountable enough. And yet, here she was, furious with a seventeen-year-old girl because she was dating her seventeen-year-old lover. He was honestly surprised the entire library didn't clue in to the obvious glare she was giving Jessica.

Tommy didn't have any delusions with Ms. Hurdtz. He didn't think she was exclusively with him or anything. She was using him for exactly the same thing he was using her for. He didn't want them to be exclusive; that'd be sick. Christ, she had to be at least thirty. But teasing her like this with Jessica always guaranteed that Gloria would come running to him soon after and schedule another "get together."

Games. Tommy loved games. He was good at them.

Gloria Hurdtz. She was good too. And when he played his game, she couldn't keep her hands off him. Let's be honest, who could resist him? He was after all, the one, the only, the fuckin' great Tommy Bates.

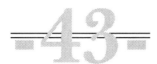

The Adult Correctional Institution is located in Cranston, Rhode Island. I do not belong in Cranston, Rhode Island. My hair does not rise a foot and a half over my head. I do not wear jewelry. I do not drink Courvoisier. I do not drive a Trans Am nor do I drive a Corvette. Or a Mercedes. And nobody in Cranston has sideburns. Nobody.

The only thing I had going for me was the fact that my friend Joe Fargnoli assured me that no one would bother me for the hour I was in town. He'd already made phone calls. If anyone did hassle me, I could reach him at Panera's. He'd be there drinking coffee. All day.

I pulled into the ACI and parked the Mustang on the small cramped patch of concrete that served as a parking lot. Around me people sat in cars smoking cigarettes, listening to the radio, or getting the kids ready to go see whichever parent was in jail. Some of the people had already started forming a line at the front door, not wanting to waste time once visiting hours started.

The ACI housed both men's and women's jails, classified in terms of maximum, high, medium, and minimum security. Lucille had issued me a pass this morning that, much to the consternation of everyone else, allowed me to cut in front of the line and be ushered right in.

Once inside, I removed my sunglasses, hung up my jacket, walked through a metal detector, and had one of the guards pat me down. I walked down the hallway with another guard, turned the corner, and stopped in front of a small room fronted with a large plate glass window. Inside the room sat a young man who I assumed to be Aaron Stanchion.

Lucille had called ahead, and as such, I was allowed to talk with Aaron in what passed for a small conference room. There would be no plate glass separating the two of us, no need for us to converse via phones or intercoms. The guard opened the door and let me know he'd be standing right outside if I needed him.

I walked into the room. Aaron was seated at the far end of a small table facing me. He was tall, with very short black hair and long, narrow hands. He was dressed in the standard-issue prison jumpsuit provided by the taxpayers of Rhode Island. He had a nervous tic in his right eye, and his right leg jiggled up and down in constant motion.

I sat down in the chair opposite Aaron.

"I know you?" he asked.

"I'd like to talk about your father."

"You know my father?"

"I work for him."

Aaron's hands remained still in front of him, but his leg continued to vibrate under the table.

"He's a fuck," Aaron said.

"He says the same thing about you."

Aaron gave a derisive snort and looked down at the table.

"It's true. Only I'm in here and he's out there."

"Should he be in here?"

Aaron snorted again.

"You work for my father. You know."

"Your father hired me to find out who killed your sister."

Aaron cocked his head as he looked at me.

"You a cop?"

"Private."

He considered that for a minute.

"What did my father tell you?"

"Your sister was shot. He wanted me to find who did it. Didn't seem to mind if I killed them in the process."

"What'd he say about me?"

"You were in jail for drugs."

Aaron grinned and looked back down at the table.

"That's right. He happen to mention the drugs were his?"

It was my turn to cock my head.

"Must've slipped his mind."

Aaron looked up and met my eyes. The grin stayed on his face.

"Dad's got a brand new Porsche. I'm a nineteen-year-old kid. Got a date. I know my chances of getting laid improve dramatically if I show up in Dad's car, and so does Dad. Dad offers to let me take his car on the date. Out of character for the old man? Absolutely. But he doesn't have to offer me twice. Whatever's moving him to be generous isn't likely to last long. He gives me the keys and I'm outta there."

The twitching in Aaron's leg sped up.

"He does ask one favor. Asks me to take the package on the dining room table and drop it off at the U-Haul storage facility in the center of town. They're open late and have a UPS drop-off center on site. I speed over there, mail the package, and come back to find two police cars waiting for me in the parking lot.

"They ask me if this is my car, and I say no, it's my dad's. They ask me to pop the trunk, which I do, and lo and behold, it's filled to the brim with drugs. Speed, hash, coke, you name it, it's there. One-stop shopping.

"Next thing I know, I'm handcuffed and in the back of one of the cruisers. Cops tell me Dad reports his car stolen and in the same breath mentions he's found drug paraphernalia in my bedroom. Says he's worried. Suspicious I could be involved in criminal activities. Cops retrieve the package I just mailed, and— surprise, surprise—it's stacked with heroin.

"Daddy-O comes down to the station and presses whatever charges he can: stolen vehicle, possession, intent to sell, whatever he can. Says it's tough love. Prick actually looks me in the face and says that."

He leaned back in his chair and looked at me. His leg slowed down.

"That's my dad."

"Your own dad set you up?"

Aaron looked at me in mock amazement.

"Fucking detective."

"Didn't you get a lawyer?"

"Do you know who my father is? He's represented the mob and he's pressing charges against his own son. Who's gonna oppose him? Everybody turned their heads. They gave me some weak-ass public defender, probably two days after taking her bar exam. I'm here, private detective. I'm here for awhile."

"I didn't see all this in the papers."

"Taken care of out of court. Dad called in some favors. Didn't want a spectacle out there, as he's planning his campaign future. Said he was embarrassed enough by his son already."

I sat back in my chair and looked at Aaron.

"You got any idea why your father would want you in jail?"

He shrugged. "Guys in here talk about Seamus Lynch. How tough he is. How he's all about loyalty. You want to be in with him, you gotta prove it. His initiation, y'know? Guys in here say one way you prove you're loyal to Lynch: You show him how important he is. More important than anything; more important than your own family. Guys in here tell stories how people sell their own mothers to impress Lynch."

"You think that's why he set you up?"

Aaron looked at me for awhile. He nodded once.

"He in with Lynch?"

Aaron shrugged and smiled. "I ain't in here 'cause I couldn't make rent."

"You think he's been dealing drugs for awhile?"

He shook his head. "That's Lynch's deal. Dad's too scared to do that. He's not bright enough either." He paused. "It's cash. Dad's not a tough guy. But he sees dollar signs wherever he can."

"And associating with Lynch can lead to power as well as money." Aaron nodded.

"Dad's a sucker."

I pulled out a folded printout of the newspaper photo showing the blond with whom Stanchion had admitted having an affair. The magic of technology allowed for multiple prints of any evidence heretofore crumpled and destroyed by distraught respondents, a true boon for detective trade. I placed the photo on the table in front of Aaron.

"You ever seen this person before?"

Aaron leaned forward, taking the photo in his hands. He studied it for a minute and then gave it back to me, shaking his head.

"No."

I folded the photo and put it back in my pocket. I stood up.

"You think of anything else that might be useful, have one of the guards contact Lieutenant Simon in Narragansett."

Aaron smiled and blew air out of his nose. "Sure, detective. We're all real tight in here. Real tight."

I turned and walked away.

"Hey detective," he called as I reached the door. "You gonna try and prove my dad's a criminal?"

I stopped and looked back at him. He was motionless in his orange jumpsuit.

"I think so."

His eyes met mine.

"Good luck."

Erin watched him get up from the bed and go into the bathroom. Her clothes were draped neatly over the hotel chair, and her gun was in the nightstand drawer, within easy reach.

So far, this was an easy job.

Michael Stanchion wasn't the most attractive man she'd been with, but she'd been with worse. Attraction didn't have anything to do with it in the first place. It was all about doing the job. Sex allowed her to get in close with him. He trusted her, he wanted her around him, he wanted her near. And those were all qualities that enabled her to do her job.

Seamus had given her a very simple directive: Watch him. Seamus was funneling quite a lot of money through Michael Stanchion. Actually, "quite a lot" was the understatement of the year. The money Stanchion was storing for Lynch could probably buy the better part of Russia.

Stanchion wasn't just storing it, either. He was delivering it. The conventions and political rallies brought together some of both Lynch's and Corey Runter's most prominent clientele. Michael's political campaign was the ideal front to use in transactions dealing with both drugs and girls. The buyers were right there and got immediate results, and the money trail was lost amidst the myriad of donations and contributions both coming and going from Stanchion's treasury.

Seamus Lynch had a good thing going. Corey Runter had made good on his promise: Seamus was reaping the benefits of a monopoly on the drug trade. Runter was also making a considerable profit controlling prostitution.

Too good a profit, Seamus had decided.

He didn't tell her this of course, but she knew. Seamus wanted to control both. He didn't want to have to share anything. Rhode Island was too small and Seamus was too arrogant. He was funneling Runter's money through Michael, but he was holding back cash for himself each time. She knew.

Seamus had hired her because he said a woman would be less visible, less suspected, and trusted more. He was right. It had worked for her in the past. It worked for her now. Anyone with half a brain knew those dressed-up bodybuilders outside were bodyguards, but no one would think the same of her.

Seamus needed to take his own advice. He paid her as a bodyguard, but when he looked at her he still just saw a woman. He let things slip in conversation with her. That's the thing with men. Their blood flow can only go in two directions, and one is directly away from the brain.

She'd pieced together enough to figure out what was going on. She was here to protect Stanchion if Runter found out what Lynch was doing. More importantly, she was here to report back to Lynch anything out of the ordinary: conversations between Michael and Corey, large cash withdrawals, arguments, suspicions, anything. She was Seamus Lynch's eyes within the confines of Michael's campaign.

Michael came back into the room and got back under the covers. She pulled him over to her, rested his head on her breasts, and stroked his hair.

"You're quiet tonight," she said.

Nothing in response.

She shifted her body so Michael was looking directly at her breasts. Eye to nipple. Redirect that blood flow.

"Want to tell me what's wrong?"

"You don't want to hear this," he said. "You don't want to hear this about me."

"Shhh." He was drunk too. This job was so easy. "Yes I do, baby." She kissed his temple. "Yes I do. You can tell me."

Michael Stanchion told Erin Oregot how he'd set his son up for a prison sentence to show his loyalty to Seamus Lynch. He'd sold one family to join another. Erin listened intently to every word and nodded sympathetically as he poured out his soul to her. Beneath her veneer, however, she had no compassion whatsoever. Seamus Lynch was a bad man. This is what happens when you deal with bad men. She was quietly thankful that she had no family Seamus could use against her.

What she really wanted to tell Michael was that this probably wasn't the last time Seamus would use his family against him.

Reality was cruel. My body had been kicked around for the last few days. I wasn't as young as I used to be. Add everything together, and upon returning home, my body rebelled against me and simply shut down.

I fell asleep on the couch, and when I awoke it was 4 p.m. the next day. The Pinkerton Agency bragged, "We never sleep." I couldn't even get away with "I only doze a little." My body felt numb and tight as I got up, and staggering into the bathroom to splash water on my face didn't help as much as I had hoped.

I didn't have enough ingredients in the kitchen to make toast, a revelation that made a return visit to the couch look even more appealing, but I rallied my strength together, pulled on a sweatshirt, and headed out to find some food. The town of Wakefield has a diner that serves breakfast around the clock, and I parked on the street, bought a copy of the paper at Healy's newsstand, and settled into a booth just after five p.m. to eat hash, eggs, and an English muffin. I tried not to let the fact that most of civilization had accomplished the very same thing twelve hours earlier bruise my ego too much.

The hash was warm, the eggs went down easy, and my body started to loosen up a bit. Everything in due time. I read through the paper as I ate my breakfast/dinner. There was still no mention of Corey Runter's death, and I was reasonably sure there wouldn't be. The South County section ran an article that stated that Michael Stanchion would be attending a convention in Washington, D.C., for the week, but would return next week, just in time for a final reception in Newport before the elections. I was pretty sure a little digging would show that there was no convention for Stanchion to be attending in D.C., and he was just providing an excuse that allowed him to lay low for a little bit. I was also pretty sure there were many more successful detectives who didn't glean their only scraps of information from reading the local paper.

I folded the paper and sat back in the booth. There were a few different ways I could play this. I could bring all the assumptions, maybes, and hypotheticals I had to the police, drop them off, and let them deal with it. I could go pound on Stanchion's door repeatedly until someone finally let me in and then hold him at gunpoint until he told me what the hell was going on. Or I could simply pack my bag, sell my house, and move to Miami Beach, where I'd just sit on the sand and toss back tequila shots every half hour until I passed out. Only one of these scenarios worked itself into any sort of image where I had a smile on my face.

I paid my tab and walked back up the street to my car. The police were overworked as it was, and going to them with a suspicion that a politician was corrupt wasn't exactly bringing up groundbreaking news in Rhode Island. I had no guarantee that Stanchion would be home, let alone in the state, and even less of a guarantee that I would be able to resist shooting him before he gave me anything I considered relevant.

The evening air was cold. I sat in the car and let the engine warm up. We had established a link between Michael Stanchion and Seamus Lynch, but Stanchion was scared. Even if I could find him, watching him was probably going to be useless. He was going to be as quiet and inconspicuous as he could.

It made sense, instead, to watch Lynch. Runter was dead and Stanchion was MIA. If anybody was going to do anything, it'd be Lynch. Might as well put an eye out on him and see where it leads. Of course, I had already been shot at twice simply by associating with a wannabe governor. Tailing and possibly interfering with a drug lord's day basically mandated my life being threatened. Not exactly encouraging.

I nosed the car out into the street and headed home.

Miami Beach still sounded very tempting.

The next morning was cold. The sky was naked and bleak and held forth with the strong promise of not getting any better. At precisely ten o'clock, freshly rejuvenated, I was sitting two parking lots away from Rudder's, keenly engrossed in noticing anyone worth noticing coming or going from Lynch's establishment. At ten twenty, my passenger-side door opened, and Graham Porter forced himself into the front seat of my car.

"Got yer message," he said after he shut the door. "What 'zactly are we doin' here?"

"Waiting."

"Waiting."

"And watching."

"Watching." He nodded. "That's your fucking plan?"

"Be nice. Took me two days to come up with this."

Graham gazed absently out the window. Two seagulls flew over the hood. A handful of cars passed by us on the main road.

"Nice inconspicuous car you've got here to sit in while you wait an' watch an' scope out the bad guys," Graham muttered. "Really, Sam. Nobody's gonna notice a Mustang parked out here fer the next twenty-four hours."

"Relax. He's two buildings away. And Lynch won't shoot at us. From his own building? In broad daylight?"

"Lynch won't. But he'll have no problem making a phone call t'someone who'll drive by an' spray us from another car."

"Spray us?"

"Gun us down."

I nodded. "You may have a point."

"Do tell."

"So glad you've got the street lingo down though."

"You're an asshole."

"Now that would be lingo that's accepted anywhere."

I drove back home, and at one-thirty Graham picked me up in a dirty, beat-up Ford F150 truck with lobster crates, nets, and buoys piled in the back.

"Put dis on," he said, and handed me a heavy-duty flannel shirt and a black watch cap. He was already dressed in a tan fisherman's sweater and had a watch cap of his own covering his enormous bald head. By two o'clock we were parked in a dirt lot across the street from the bar, two front-row seats looking straight at the front door.

"This won't be noticed?" I asked. "Graham, we're fifty feet away from the front door. Put the truck in neutral and we'll roll right into the damn bar."

"Trust me, Sammy. We're two fishermen sitting in a truck full o' equipment. We blend right in. For all anybody cares, we took the day off, we're drinkin' beers, we don't wanna go home to the wives. No one notices."

"Where'd you get the truck?"

"Don't ask."

"Uh-huh. And if somebody does get suspicious and runs the plates?"

"Plates belong to the optometrist who lives three doors down from me. Asked me t'keep an eye on his home while he's on vacation. I'll have the plates back on his Beamer before his plane touches the ground. Assumin', dat is, you find a clue sometime soon while we out here in disguise."

"Don't push me. I'm just starting to get good at this."

Graham grunted as he settled into his seat. "Let me know when you improve."

"Hell," I said, "I'm hoping you'll tell me."

It took much longer than it should have. Of course, I hold with the assumption that the world would run much more efficiently if everyone worked off of my schedule. Graham and I stayed in the truck two hours past when we couldn't see anything in the dark and came up with zilch. The following day I was the sole idiot sitting on the outside deck of a neighboring restaurant in the chill November air. I stalled for three and a half hours while eating my lunch—very slowly and with multiple courses—but the only action at Rudder's was deliveries from two different beer trucks. Graham spent the night inside the tavern, sitting at the bar, and while he, too, reported nothing out of the ordinary, he accompanied Julia the bartender back home for the night. All things considered, so far he was having more success than I was in this venture.

We spent the next day back in the truck. Graham had emptied all the fishing gear out of the back and decided to park on the street by a telephone pole four blocks away. He then pulled six orange cones out of the back and placed them around the truck, giving us a six-foot berth in front and in back.

"We're state workers today, Sam," he said, climbing back in. "Ain't nobody gonna question what we're doin' out here."

He picked up his Styrofoam cup and drank some coffee.

"Seamus gonna give you a hard time, he finds out you're helping me watch him?" I asked.

Graham looked sideways at me. "Who in their right mind gonna try an' give me a hard time?"

"True. Let me rephrase the question. Am I upsetting an established respect by having you side with me against Lynch?"

Graham shook his head and placed his cup back in the truck's cup holder.

"I don't take sides. Seamus knows that. He finds out I'm helpin' you and he wants me to stop, he knows all he has to do is offer me more money than you offerin'."

"With what I'm offering, pal, he could buy you off with food stamps."

"I realize dat. I even have to buy my own coffee." He twisted in his seat to look at me. "This ain't about money, Sammy. Seventeen-year-old girl got murdered, and it a pretty safe bet she ain't done nuthin' t'deserve that. From what I unnerstan', she a real sweet girl."

For a moment I wondered how old Annabeth would have been if she were alive.

"Plenty o' people aroun' who should be popped in the head," Graham continued. "Not her. Shouldn'ta happened."

"No," I agreed. "It shouldn'ta."

Michael Stanchion stood in the parking lot and looked at the dilapidated structure in front of him. The roof rose and fell with a mind of its own. The neon sign blinked haphazardly in a threatening Morse code, and the windows were covered in grime that strangled any light trying to get in or out of the building.

Michael stared at this bar called Mulligan's. Did he really have to enter this godforsaken place? Yes he did if he wanted to move forward in life. The type of people he would meet inside this place were the type of people who would do what he needed right now. He didn't like it, but the sooner he put it in motion, the sooner he could put it behind him.

His partnership with Seamus was flourishing. The money they were stealing from Corey was being redirected in avenues that would very quietly build an empire over which Seamus and he could rule. Michael wasn't stupid. Of course he knew Lynch was using him as a front to skim money from Runter. Seamus didn't deny it when Michael confronted him with it, and the only thing Michael chided him for was not stealing enough.

Together they devised multiple routes through which they could deposit the money, slowly depleting Runter of his funds, which would in turn remove him from the power structure. Worked correctly, Stanchion's office would do nothing but aid Lynch. Stanchion, firmly entrenched in both the State House and Seamus Lynch's enterprises, stood poised to become one of the most dominating presences in the northeast.

Stanchion liked the idea. He wasn't worried about Lynch threatening or blackmailing him once he was in office. He had enough to hold over Lynch's head if it came to that. The lawyer side of him had made sure he gathered that information. No, he wasn't worried. He was quickly becoming a power player himself.

The only loose end was Erin. He had told her what he'd done to his son. If she wanted to, she could make enough noise to bring on an investigation. The possibility of a scandal could not be tolerated. One investigation would lead to another and then another. Enough scrutiny would eventually uncover something that could hurt him.

Of course, Erin might not make any noise. She might settle for being paid off. Or she might not say anything at all. She seemed to like him. But Michael couldn't wager his future on what Erin might or might not do. And he refused to begin his political career already paying off one potential blackmailer.

That left one alternative.

Sally the Whore had told him of Max. Max is the best, she said. Nobody sees Max coming or going, she said. You want someone dead for sure, go to Max. No mess, no trace, she said. Michael was at Mulligan's to meet someone who would put him in contact with Max. Max would take care of Erin. Without Erin there would be no loose ends. Nothing to worry about. Nothing to hold him back.

Michael took a look at the structure in front of him.

This Mulligan's really is a godforsaken place.

He took a deep breath and walked forward.

Godforsaken.

He opened the door and stepped inside.

On the fourth day we hit pay dirt.

Lil and I were in her Jeep, parked in a loading dock on the side of an ice plant at the end of the bar's street. The ice trucks had already left with their deliveries for the day, and, it being November, I didn't foresee much foot traffic coming in and out of a building where the room temperature was below thirty degrees. Lil, noting that we hadn't seen each other in a week, had decided to join me, and as such, at noontime we were firmly encapsulated in her Jeep, Subway sandwiches in hand, on the lookout for anything that qualified as nefarious activity.

"So let's see," she began. "I've spent time with you sitting in a car watching a teenager's house, sitting in a car watching a hotel entranceway, and now I'm sitting in a car with you looking at a bar."

"Our life together gets too exciting, let me know."

It didn't get much more stimulating than that for the better part of the afternoon. Then, at three o'clock, a gold Karmann Ghia convertible pulled into the parking lot, and out stepped the tall blond woman who had formerly been identified as Michael Stanchion's campaign mistress. Her curly blond hair fell to her shoulders, and she pulled the belt of her black-as-night trench coat tight about her waist as she strode to the front door of the bar and entered.

"Ah-ha!" I said out loud.

"Ah-ha?"

"That woman, babe, is a tangible, bona fide, no-shit-it's-for-real clue."

"The blond in the little sports car?"

"Yep."

"About fucking time." She took a sip of her coffee, which I was sure had to be cold by now, but she didn't seem to mind. "So what do we do?"

"We wait."

"Wait?"

"And see what she does."

"She just walked into the bar."

"Yes. Hopefully she'll do more."

The blond was in there for over an hour, and by the time she came out, the streetlights were starting to come on. She got back into her car, and as she did so, Lil turned the Jeep's engine over. The blond pulled out onto the road, Lil followed suit, and I made a mental note to ask Graham how inconspicuous he thought a Karmann Ghia was in Narragansett, Rhode Island.

The Ghia headed north up Route 108. Lil followed in the Jeep.

"Think you'll be able to keep up?" I asked.

"Darling. Please."

The blond drove onto Route 1 and merged onto Route 4. Lil did a good job of staying with her but not too close to her, a feat made even more admirable as it was rapidly getting darker outside. I thought we might almost lose her when we merged onto Route 95, but the traffic was just congested enough to help us out.

The blond got off in Providence and we followed. Much to the irritation of other drivers, Lil had to run two red lights to stay behind her, but this was enough of a commonplace occurrence in Providence that the angry honking of horns blended in with the rest of the background noise of the city. We circled through the city for five minutes, and the Karmann Ghia pulled into the parking lot of a club located on a corner next to a bank. Lil drove around the loop for another five minutes and then parked a block in front of the club.

The club was an old-fashioned jazz joint named Ginger's. There was a shotgun bar along the left wall as you walked in, and an assortment of high tables and chairs stood off to your right. A stage faced us from the far end of the room, where a drummer, bassist, and trumpet player worked soft, mellow tunes as they warmed up. The lights were dim, and actual candles had been placed in glass holders along the walls. Smoking was not allowed in Rhode Island restaurants, but in here it should have been encouraged.

We walked in through the front door and took a table in the far corner. No one looked up as we did so. Lil was dressed in a pair of slacks and an off-white oversized sweater with an oversized turtleneck top. I had on a black leather jacket over a black crewneck sweater and jeans. I was sure there was a dress code here, but I didn't think we'd qualify to be thrown out.

Two other couples sat at tables around the room. The blond was sitting at the corner of the bar sipping a drink, her midnight black raincoat draped carefully over her chair. A large man was leaning over the bar talking intently to the bartender. The bartender cleaned a glass and listened while the man talked. When he was finished, he stood up and turned to the blond. The large man was Horace Zile. He nodded once to the blond, who gave no indication she even knew he was standing there, and then turned abruptly and walked out.

"The plot thickens," I said.

"Oh, we know him, don't we?" said Lil.

A cocktail waitress came over to take our order. The blond didn't look like she was in a hurry to go anywhere, so neither were we. I ordered a gin and tonic, and Lil ordered a beer.

"Beer?"

"Irish."

"True."

The band continued to warm up, and a girl in a silver gown came out and started to sing. She didn't have the smoky, raspy voice of a blues singer, but rather the taut, wiry voice that goes with jazz. She finished one song and started a second. The waitress returned with our drinks and I paid her.

"I like a woman who drinks beer."

"You'd like a woman who drinks detergent," Lil said, watching the band.

The blond turned around in her seat and rested her elbow on the bar as she watched the musicians. The band wasn't playing to anybody; they were just jamming together to work out some numbers for this evening. They'd stop, restart, laugh, fool around, all of which made it more intimate for the small crowd that was present. The blond turned to the bartender, ordered another drink, and then resumed watching the band. She seemed very content.

"This reminds me of that place we went to when we were in New York on Christmas Eve."

"Milo's? Lounge singer was a bisexual transvestite who sang folk music."

"No, that was where we had dinner. I'm talking about where we went afterwards and heard an entire band." She raised her glass to her lips and drank some beer. "So what's the deal with her?" Lil asked, motioning towards the blond.

"Not sure."

"But she's important?"

"Think so."

"What's her name?"

"Couldn't tell you."

Lil looked at me.

"I take it there's no exam for you to renew your investigator's license."

"Woman had an affair with Stanchion, woman worked on his campaign, woman walked into Lynch's bar. Seems to be a good reason to see where she goes."

"So for now we just sit here and listen to jazz."

"Yep."

"And you're calling this work."

"Enjoy. It's the closest we've come to a date this week."

The band went through five more songs. Six more people floated into the bar in the course of a half hour; two couples who wound up at tables and two patrons who found ample space at the bar. The noise never got too loud, in clubs like this it never does.

The blond had nursed her second drink. When her glass was finally empty, she set it down squarely on the napkin in front of her, picked her purse up off the bar, and stood up and headed for the ladies' room. Lil saw her and did the same. Within a minute, Lil walked back out of the ladies' room, carrying the blond's pearl-white purse.

"Let's go," she said.

We exited the club and walked back to Lil's Jeep. I got in the driver's side and started up the engine. We pulled away from the curb and Lil started rummaging through the purse.

"You do make yourself useful," I said.

"Never leave your purse by the sink. Always take it with you into the stall. Cardinal rule."

"She see you?"

"That question is so stupid, I'm not even going to dignify it with an answer." Lil pulled items from the purse. "Woman travels light but practical. We have gum, lipstick, compact, nail polish, oh look, a gun, hairbrush, condoms, and a passport."

"What's the name on the passport?"

Lil returned the other items to the purse and opened the passport.

"Erin Maxine Oregot."

Graham had never seen the blond in the picture before, nor did the name Erin Maxine Oregot ring a bell. He was, however, familiar with the jazz club Ginger's.

"Lynch owns the club. He don't like keepin' his money in one place so he moves it around all the time. Dat way he always has access to it, but nobody knows how much is where."

"The man own every bar in the state?"

"Naw, only three, s'far as I know. But I know he sends guys diff'rent places t'get paid after a job."

"You ever been to Ginger's?" I asked.

"Nope. Lynch deals with me direct. This here's a field trip."

It was just after three on Wednesday afternoon, and we were heading back up to Providence via Route 95. Ray Charles was singing "Unchain My Heart" through my car's stereo system.

"I like this guy," Graham said.

"Hard not to."

I had seen the bartender at Ginger's speak with Horace, and Horace had acknowledged Erin before he left. Someone in that group had to have an idea of what the hell was going on. The easiest way to get an answer would be to simply ask, and the easiest person to get a hold of was the bartender. Graham said he'd come along and help out in case anything got lost in translation.

"You've been spending a lot of time with me over the last week," I said. "How's this affecting your other forms of income?"

"Cash flow not a problem," Graham said.

Good to know.

Ginger's didn't open to the public until three. No lunch business here. Music seven nights a week, but the band didn't officially go on until nine. It was three thirty when we parked in the lot. The street was lined with the cars of people at work for the day, but ours was the only car parked at the club. At least we wouldn't have to wait for a drink.

Graham had on a black sweater, jeans, and work boots. I was wearing similar colors in the form of a black T-shirt, jeans, and a black leather jacket, but somehow I didn't think people would mistake us for twins. A steady wind blew across the parking lot as we walked to the front door. Graham didn't seem affected by the cold.

"Think anybody will mistake us for twins?" I asked.

Graham just looked at me.

The bar was the same dimly lit room it had been yesterday, and the gentleman working the bar was the same man who had been working yesterday. I love consistency. No one from the band had set up yet, and a lone patron sat at the far end of the bar by the stage. Graham and I walked in and sat down.

"What'll it be, gentlemen?" the bartender asked as he walked down our way. He was dressed in a tuxedo shirt and tie and had a paper-thin mustache he'd probably been trying to grow for the last year. He finished wiping the glass he was carrying, stacked it back on the shelf, and rested his forearms on the bar in front of us.

"I'd like to speak with Horace Zile," I said.

The bartender straightened up. "Who?" he asked. He glanced over at Graham and then quickly looked away. Graham was quietly resting his forearms on the bar as well, but his forearms were decidedly larger. This fact did not seem to be lost on the bartender.

"Horace Zile," I repeated. "Hard name to forget."

"Don't know anybody by that name, sir."

"Yes you do. You spoke with him yesterday. Large man, looks like a clean-shaven ape. After he was done talking with you, he nodded goodbye to the knockout who was sitting down the other end of the bar."

He shook his head. "Sorry, sir. You must be mistaken."

Graham reached over the bar and grabbed the front of the bartender's shirt with both hands. Without any visible effort at all he hoisted him up and over the bar and placed him on the bar stool between the two of us. The bartender's mouth was open when Graham put him down on the stool, and it wasn't until after he looked at the two of us that he remembered to close it. A thin sheen of sweat had formed over his upper lip, and I was afraid it would wilt his attempt at a mustache before our conversation was finished. Graham kept one mammoth hand planted on the bartender's shoulder.

"Refresh yer memory," he said.

"Don't wrinkle his shirt," I said. "His shift just started."

I glanced over at the patron at the other end of the bar. He saw this as an opportune time to utilize the facilities in the men's room and was walking over in that direction. I turned back to the bartender.

"Hey man, c'mon, ease up," he said. "I can't go around spillin' everything to anybody who comes in off the street, y'know?" Graham squeezed his shoulder. "C'mon man, really. Mr. Lynch'll kill me."

"If he finds out," I said. "Who's gonna tell? He's not here. Give us something or we'll hurt you now."

He was scared. I sounded tough. Of course it was easy to sound tough when I had a man who could bench-press my car holding onto my captive's right arm.

"I—I don't know how to get in touch with Mr. Zile," he said. "He just shows up. Honest. I swear."

"What was he doing here yesterday?"

His eyes were wide; whether from fear or pain I couldn't tell.

"Dro-dropping off money," he stammered. "For Max. That's all I know. Really."

Graham looked up. "Max is workin' fer Lynch?"

"I don't know. I don't even know who Max is. I was just told to make the money available for three days. After three days Mr. Zile will come back." He stopped as soon as he said that. He looked at us. "Please don't be here waiting for Mr. Zile. Please don't tell him I said anything. He'll kill me."

"Anybody come for the money yet?" I asked.

He shook his head.

"OK," I said. "Thank you." Graham and I stood up. The other patron poked his head out of the men's room, saw we were still there, and went back in. I took a twenty out of my wallet and put it on the bar. The bartender remained slumped on the bar stool.

"Mr. Lynch ain't gonna find out we talked, is he?" he asked.

"You plan on tellin' him?" Graham asked.

He shook his head. "No."

"All right, then."

He was still slumped on the stool when we left.

"So who's Max?"

We were battling traffic as we headed back down to Narragansett. It was the onset of rush hour and cars were bumper to bumper. We were losing the battle.

"Shooter. Best shooter dere is, actually. If Lynch is workin' with Max, he wants somebody gone quickly an' quietly an' without a mess."

"Stanchion?"

"I wuz thinkin' you."

"Me? But we got along so well the last time we spoke."

Graham snorted. "Go figure."

I shrugged. "At least my price went up."

"Price," Graham said. "Not value."

"Yeah, but I'm annoying enough to warrant paying top dollar."

"There is dat."

I crept over to the high-speed lane, where the traffic allowed me to gun it at 30 mph.

"You ever meet Max?" I asked.

Graham shook his head. "Uh-uh. Just know 'im by reputation."

"And I assume he's not listed in the Yellow Pages. How does one find him?"

"I know you can reach him through Mulligan's," Graham said. "Just gotta put up half the dough ahead o' time; show you're serious. Although nobody stupid enough to renege payin' a shooter. Signin' your own death warrant, ya do that. Max then take three days, like the man said, t'scope out the job. If Max don't want it, you get yer money back."

"A killer with a conscience?"

"Killer who don't wanna get caught. He don't care who he's shootin'. He cares who's hirin' him. Too easy fer anyone t'walk inta Mulligan's an' put down some cash; say yer lookin' fer Max. Wants t'make sure nobody's settin' him up. His own sorta background check."

"Pretty good bet Seamus isn't working undercover for the FBI."

"Yeah, but Max is a package deal. Same rules apply, no matter who you are. Three days is three days is three days. His way of stayin' in charge. Once he signs on, though, you're dead."

"Well isn't that lovely."

We were quiet while we digested that thought. The radio was off and the heater was on low. We drove along in silence, and I reviewed the events of the past twenty-four hours. We had watched Erin Oregot enter Lynch's bar and remain in there for about an hour. We'd followed her to Ginger's whereupon we found Horace Zile, who, according to the bartender, was dropping off money for Max. Horace had nodded at Erin before leaving.

Graham jerked his head off the headrest and looked at me. He'd reached the same conclusion I had at the same time.

"The blond at the bar. What was her full name?" he asked.

"Erin Maxine Oregot."

"Maxine."

"Maxine." I glanced at Graham. "You've never actually seen Max?"

"Nope. Never."

"Matter of fact, only thing we know about Max is that Max is the best shooter around."

"That's all we know."

I looked out the windshield at the line of cars that stretched out infinitely in front of me.

"Nothing in the rule book that says the best shooter around can't be a gorgeous blond with incredible legs."

"Nothin' at all," Graham agreed. "Lucky we two liberated men so's we can figger out our shooter's a she, not a he."

"I'm no sexist. I'm equally against anybody shooting at me, male or female."

"'Course, we could be jumpin' to conclusions here. Blond mighta just been at the bar 'cause she likes jazz."

"Or she could have seen me walk in," I said, "and she just wanted to sit, stare, and fantasize about me for awhile."

Graham looked at me.

"OK, so we in full agreement then that she's the shooter, and now we know who to be lookin' for t'be pointin' a gun at you."

"Well, if you want to dismiss my theory, yes."

I took the exit for Route 4, and traffic started to thin out a little.

"You see this as a good thing," I said. "We now have to be wary of every blond who happens to look over in my general direction."

"Don't worry," Graham said, leaning back and closing his eyes. "Won't be that many."

So easy.

Erin Oregot counted the bills one more time.

So easy.

Michael Stanchion—Michael fucking Stanchion—had gone to Mulligan's himself and put down cash to hire her. This entire world was a joke.

Of course Michael didn't know that she and Max were the same person. The only person who could inform him of that fact was Seamus, and there was absolutely no reason for Seamus to do that. She did wonder how Michael had come to know of Max, but Michael wasn't so clean-cut that he wouldn't know people who could point him in the direction of a killer if he needed one.

She checked the date again. She was attending a function with Michael the night he was hiring her to shoot someone. A minor conflict. She could easily come up with an excuse to leave early without him. Perhaps she'd encourage him to invite his wife to this affair. That would give her a reason to vanish.

She smiled to herself as she put the money away.

So easy.

Like shooting ducks in a barrel.

The only person of relevance I had not talked with was Stanchion's wife, Vanessa. Even though I didn't believe for a minute that Michael Stanchion was in D.C., I didn't think he was stupid enough to try and stay in hiding in his own home. A quick call to Mrs. Stanchion confirmed that as fact, and a time was set to meet early that afternoon.

I didn't know how receptive Vanessa would be to talking to me alone, so I brought Lil with me to break the ice. Lil could be very warm and accommodating when she wanted to. At least that's what she promised me.

Mrs. Stanchion seemed to attend many of the functions her husband did. She also seemed to play the role of the detached observer when she was at them. My hopes were that in talking with her we would stumble upon some piece of information that she didn't realize she'd picked up at one of her outings. Maybe she had seen someone or heard something that would help us figure out where Stanchion was headed next. Of course, the possibility that I was being watched by a shooter for an opportune time to cap my ass also gave forth the chance that I was putting the lives of two innocent people at risk. My job was not without its moral dilemmas.

The driveway contained both cars, the Jag and the Subaru, and for a moment I wondered if Vanessa was trying to set us up. She greeted us at the door alone, however, and ushered us into what appeared to be an otherwise empty house. We sat in the living room, and the sunlight streamed in from a large bay window. There was nothing extravagant in the way of décor, and the furniture gave a cozy and familial atmosphere to the room.

Lil and I sat on a green love seat up against the far wall. Vanessa drew the shades to blot out the sun and took a seat opposite us in one of two upright chairs. She had a pitcher of lemonade and glasses on the coffee table, and I poured us each a glass.

Mrs. Stanchion looked very small in the chair. She sat upright, with her feet flat on the floor and her hands in her lap. Her eyes were wide and seemed to be searching and waiting at the same time. We were all quiet for a minute. The room was still. Vanessa finally broke the silence.

"Is Michael in trouble?" She said the words slowly, as if she had spent the morning composing and practicing the question.

"We're hoping you can help us figure that out, Mrs. Stanchion," I said. "Do you have any reason to believe that he is?"

"Well…I don't know. He's just been working so hard, and then he left for the week, and now you're coming around asking questions…"

"Where is your husband now?" Lil asked gently.

"He's up in Maine. Took the train Sunday night. He said he wanted to just get away for a bit before the final rally this weekend."

"The election's almost here and he picks now to take a vacation? You don't find that a little strange?" I asked. Lil gave me a look that said *calm down*.

Mrs. Stanchion sunk back into her chair. "I…I never thought of it that way. I guess I just thought he needed a rest. He's been working so hard."

"Why did he go to Maine?" I asked.

"We have a cabin there," she replied. "Nothing much, just a two-bedroom cottage. We use it to get away. Michael can't leave his work alone unless he's physically removed from it. We used to take.....the kids up during the summer."

I waited while she composed herself.

"He's up there now?"

She nodded. "He said he just needed a couple days to himself. Just to get away from everything. He's coming back Friday night, and the reception is on Saturday." She looked at me. "He doesn't show it, Mr. Miller, but he's really been in anguish over the events of the past month."

"My thoughts are with both of you," I said. I paused. "Did your husband ever mention the name Corey Runter, Mrs. Stanchion?" I asked. "Or Seamus Lynch?"

She shook her head.

"How about Erin Oregot?"

At the mention of Erin's name she flushed briefly and looked down at her hands.

"I know what you're insinuating, Mr. Miller, but that escapade is over. Ms. Oregot no longer works with my husband. He got rid of her."

"He doesn't see her anymore?" I asked. "You believe that?"

"He fired her," she said. She looked up and there were tears in her eyes. "My husband loves me, Mr. Miller."

I started to say something but Lil put her hand on my leg. "Please don't think we're rude, Mrs. Stanchion," she said. "We're just trying to put all the pieces together to make sure nobody's in danger."

"Who's in danger?"

"Your husband associates with some less-than-savory individuals, Mrs. Stanchion. Corey Runter and Seamus Lynch are dangerous men. Working with them puts him in danger, which means you could be in jeopardy as well."

Vanessa shook her head as if there was a buzzing in her ear. "I don't know who these people are."

I took in a deep breath and let it out slowly.

"Have you seen your son since he was put in jail, Mrs. Stanchion?"

"No I haven't," she answered. "Michael forbids it."

"I visited him," I said. "I talked with him. He seems pretty convinced that your husband set him up, put him in jail on purpose."

Vanessa Stanchion met my gaze. There were no longer tears in her eyes. "That is a lie, Mr. Miller. An outright lie." She spoke in clear, even tones now. "I will not sit here and listen to you slander my family's name in my own home."

"Vanessa, I'm not saying these things to you out of meanness. Your husband is a bad man. He's mixed up with men who are even worse. He's going to get hurt. I'm trying to prevent that. Most importantly, I'm trying to make sure you don't get caught in the crossfire."

Vanessa Stanchion stood up. "My husband is a very good man, Mr. Miller. He has been under a tremendous amount of stress since our daughter was killed. It's a wonder he even gets out of bed in the morning. As for our son, he flushed his life down the toilet. That was his decision, Mr. Miller. I assure you no one put him up to that, least of all my husband. I deal with that fact every day, wondering where I failed him as a mother, wondering what I could have done to prevent this from happening. But I will not stand here and listen to you defame my husband or take the tragedies of my family and throw them in my face." She looked away from me. "I think it is time for you to leave."

I set my empty glass down on the coffee table and sat back in the couch. I glanced at Lil. She shook her head. I blew out some air.

"Mrs. Stanchion, believe me, please, I am only looking out for your best interests." I took out a card and place it on the coffee table. "If you need me for anything, please call me. Any hour."

Her voice was a hoarse, dying whisper. "Please get out of my house." She wouldn't look at me.

We let ourselves out.

Once in awhile this job allowed me to help someone. To find a missing loved one, to clear an innocent person, to right a wrong, to mete justice, to avenge a wrongdoing. Once in awhile. More often, this job allowed me a front-row seat to the underside of humanity. The filth, the garbage, the waste, the dirt.

Being good at this job meant you had to wade through the diseased side of humanity. You had to seek it out. Walk amidst it. Pick through it. You had to be a part of it without becoming a part of it.

It gets so you're more familiar with the underbelly of humanity than the positive side. You start to question whether it's there because you're always looking for it, or you see it so easily because it's always there.

The lousy side of humanity. The dirt. A lot of people don't want to see it. They know it's there—they live in it for chrissakes—but they don't want to see it. Their way of staying clean.

I had reached a point in my life where I could take a thousand showers and the dirt still wouldn't come off. Mrs. Stanchion just didn't want to see it.

"Well that went well," Lil said as we pulled out of the driveway.

"She doesn't want to see the dirt."

"Most people don't," she replied. "They can't handle it. Doesn't mean it's not there."

I turned on the radio. Lenny Kravitz was halfway through "Stand by My Woman." Lil reached over and switched it off.

"The dirt is a part of life, Samuel." She had a point to make. When she had a point to make she talked until she was finished, and God help anyone who tried to interrupt her. "It's always been there. Always has and always will be. The survivors are the ones who recognize the dirt and flourish anyway, in spite of it. They fight against it. You are a part of the dirt, Samuel. You shake hands with it and embrace it when it serves your purpose, and you stand against it and kick it down when it needs to be. And it's a good thing too, because if it wasn't for the dirt, I wouldn't be here."

"You're not dirt, babe."

"No, but I come from it." She stopped for a moment while she collected her thoughts. We drove along the water in silence for a bit before she resumed again. "These people like Vanessa Stanchion won't have full lives." I started to say something but she cut me off. "Don't misinterpret me," she said, shaking her head. "I'm not saying she would be better off if all of the sudden she got a dark side or started committing criminal acts. But by not admitting these things are present in her life, or refusing to believe they're there, or whatever the hell she's doing, she's tying herself to her husband and allowing him to lead her blindly down the road. If she would at least acknowledge the bad stuff, then she'd have to make a conscious choice about how to react to it. Then her life would be her own, instead of spending it living in fear or denial or —"

"Pockets of chosen reality," I finished for her.

"Yes, thank you. Pockets of chosen reality."

I grinned. "You gonna start practicing therapy now?"

"They don't let you beat the patients." She looked out the window. "There's so much out there, Samuel. Some of these people don't know where to go. They're so scared."

"You got out of the dirt."

"With your help."

I shook my head slightly. "You would've gotten out anyway."

She turned to me and smiled. "But it wouldn't have been as much fun."

We drove along Ocean Road. The sky was a clear blue, and the sun was bright. Three people jogged along the water. They all wore sweatshirts that read "URI Crew Team." An elderly couple was bundled up and holding hands as they walked their dog down the sidewalk. There didn't seem to be much dirt in this corner of the universe. I turned up Knowlesway and passed a giant church building on the corner. I turned right at the light and drove up Route 108.

"Can I turn the radio back on?" I asked.

Lil continued to look out the window as we drove.

"No."

Knowing that my shooter was Max/Maxine didn't mean I automatically knew where she was or when she was going to start shooting. Lil and I had seen her go into Lynch's bar, which meant she had probably already decided to take the job. Lucky me.

Still, if what Graham said held true, I had one more day of freedom before Max officially started the job. Stanchion wasn't coming home till later tonight, Lil was working, and I didn't consider myself close enough friends with Seamus Lynch to invite him out to lunch. My three most workable scenarios now proven impractical, I decided to take myself out to the gym. My only other alternative was getting a head start on Max and hiding under the bed this afternoon instead of tomorrow morning.

I parked the car and walked to the front entrance. Even though I was reasonably confident Max would hold to her three-day standard, I still couldn't help feeling as if I had a huge bull's-eye painted on my back as I made my way across the parking lot. Once inside, however, the windowless cinder-block walls offered a much more secure feeling of protection than the open space outside. If Max did follow me in, I figured I'd notice her before she dropped a weight on my head or tried to strangle me with a jump rope.

The owner of the gym, Moira, had recently added a second floor to the gym, making room for aerobics classes and spin cycles, but the ground floor remained a weight room. I waited as my eyes adjusted to the halogen lighting and listened to the steady clang of weights as they were lifted and set down. Moira's gym was spotless and old-fashioned. No air-pressure machines, no hydraulic aids. When you worked out in Moira's gym, you earned your workout, and the sounds inside were a reminder of that. It was quietly reassuring.

Lita Ford was belting out "Kiss Me Deadly" over the sound system as I walked to the reception desk. Moira was seated behind it and was barely able to see over the desktop. A woman standing by one of the cable machines called over asking her to turn down the music. Moira grinned at me and turned up the volume.

"No, no, I asked could you turn it *down*," the woman called over again.

Moira nodded and waved her off. She ignored the volume.

"Isn't the customer always right?" I asked.

"I like this song." Moira looked up at me from behind her desk. She smiled ear to ear. "Don't you?"

"Always have."

"You're right. And you're a customer."

"Point proven. I'll explain it to her if she's still complaining later."

"I'm keeping the volume up. If she's still complaining later I won't be able to hear her."

"Such a smart girl."

"Don't forget it. You here to work out, or just stopping by to say hello?"

"I was thinking about doing a sit-up."

"Cheers. So long as you stay away from the jump rope, I don't care what you do."

"You got a problem with the way I jump rope?"

"Last time you were here, two people filed complaints about the way you were swinging that thing. One woman said she felt accosted when she walked by you."

"Accosted?"

"Accosted."

"You actually let people in here who use the word 'accosted' when referring to exercise equipment?"

"I'll take their money. Enjoy your workout. Try not to accost anyone while you're in here."

With the lighting and the music, Moira's gym could double as a night club, an added bonus to working out here. I worked out for a little over an hour and then departed for the locker room and a hot shower. Ever mindful of my situation, I asked Moira to come running if she heard any screaming coming from the shower stall. Ever mindful of her role in my life, Moira elucidated that vacating her chair for any reason, especially one involving me, would definitely result in screaming on my part, and not in a pleasurable manner.

After I finished cleaning up I drove down to Sonny's to take myself out for an early dinner. Danielle's shift didn't start till later, and I was waited on by a short, thin girl with a southern accent. She didn't smile, barely talked, and acted as if it was an imposition to dare to sit at her bar and order food. If this was to be my Last Supper, my company was up to par. I treated myself to a half-pound hamburger with extra mashed potatoes, an order my waitress took and delivered with audible sighs, showing her great distaste at expending effort of any kind. As I ate my meal, a small part of me hoped Max started shooting early and maybe, just maybe, accidentally hit my waitress in the process. At least it would save me from having to leave her a tip.

I finished my meal, paid my tab, and drove home in the twilight. When I arrived back at my house, the last vestiges of sunlight had disappeared. All the lights were on in my house, and Lil's Jeep was in my driveway. I parked on the street, walked up the stairs, and let myself in.

"Thought I told you it might be a good idea to steer clear of me for the next couple days."

"And I'm glad to see you too." Lil placed the book she was reading facedown on the coffee table and leaned back in her chair and crossed her legs. "Probably be a good idea for me to steer clear of you for more than a few days. People who know you have recommended months. Probably be in your best interests to shut your goddamn mouth and come over here and give me a kiss."

"Understood," I said and walked over and kissed her lightly on the mouth. I walked into the hallway and hung my jacket up in the closet. I came back into the kitchen and poured myself a glass of water.

"You want anything?" I asked.

Lil smiled and shook her head. I walked back into the living room and sat down on the couch. Lil tucked her feet under her and sat next to me.

"House is full of windows, babe," I said, "and you've got every single light on. Are you trying to give our shooter as much help as possible? Or are you just trying to run up my electric bill?"

"Your house can be so dreary with the lights off." She rested her head on my shoulder. "Besides we have nothing to worry about tonight. We saw Max walk into Seamus's on Tuesday afternoon. Graham said Max always takes three days to scope out a deal. That's Wednesday, Thursday, and tonight. We won't have anything to worry about until 12:01. And by that time, the lights will be off. I promise."

"You're putting a lot of faith in what Graham says."

"I put a lot of faith in Graham, period. What he says shouldn't be any different."

"Hell of a way to test a theory."

"It's not a test."

I nodded and drank some water.

"Sticking with water tonight?" she asked.

"Might be in my best interests to be exceedingly vigilant come 12:01," I said.

"Mm-hmm," Lil murmured. "I would have to agree."

We sat on the couch for a couple minutes, not saying anything. The atmosphere could have been tense, but instead was a patient waiting as thoughts surfaced.

"Are you upset I'm here?" Lil asked, breaking the silence. Before I could answer, she added, "I'm not leaving."

I shook my head. "Part of me is thrilled you're here. Beats the hell out of staring at the ceiling until tomorrow. But there's also a strong part of me that would be incredibly agitated if you were to get shot because you were here."

"Nice to hear."

"And the realistic part of me," I continued, "realizes that there's no force on the planet that could move you out of here once you've made the decision to come over and stay with me."

She smiled. "Smart boy."

"I hear that a lot."

Lil sat up and took a drink of my water. "I come bearing gifts as well," she said, and looked at me. "Michael Stanchion's big event is in Newport tomorrow night, as we know. Yours truly scored two invitations this afternoon."

"How?"

"Girl whose house I'm selling knows a guy who knows a guy."

She smiled.

I smiled.

"That's very nice," I said, "but what if I already have plans for tomorrow night?"

"Tomorrow night's Saturday. You never have plans. Trust me. I know."

I smiled again and gave her a kiss.

"You never cease to amaze," I said. "You always come through."

"Damn straight."

"A good part of me is still angry you're here. You're putting your life at risk for no good reason."

"No good reason..." She shook her head. "My choice to be here," she answered. "Not yours. You could just say thank you and shut the fuck up."

"Thank you," I said. "For the help and for coming over."

"There are times we are a 'we' Samuel, and times when we are a 'you' and a 'me.' This is one of the times when we're a 'we.'" She kissed me on the mouth. "Now come with me," she said, taking my hand. "There are circumstances where staring at the ceiling can be more pleasurable than you realize."

I awoke to the smell of frying bacon and the sound of voices coming from another room. I pulled on a pair of jeans and walked into my kitchen to find Lil talking with Graham. He grinned when he saw me.

"Daylight outside," he said, "and look at dis brave bastard come walkin' right inta his own livin' room. No Fear Charley, dat's him."

He was dressed simply in a T-shirt and jeans, but the T-shirt strained visibly against his massive body.

"I planned on crawling under the couch for safety," I said, leaning against the doorjamb, "but now that you're here, I might just walk behind you and let you get shot first."

"I ain't gonna get shot," Graham smiled. "I gets along wit' ev'rybody. You the one goin' out an' annoyin' all the wrong people in dis town."

"Yeah, well at least my T-shirts fit me."

Graham shrugged. "You do get points fer bein' the world's scrawniest target, I'll give you that." He sat down at my kitchen table.

"Want some breakfast?" Lil asked. She smiled brilliantly. "We can set you up in the hallway if you'd like."

She placed three eggs and two pieces of bacon on a plate and handed it to Graham.

I sat down at the table myself. "You can both go to hell." Graham had positioned the table so I was sitting in the corner. His frame blocked the vantage point of the sliding-glass door in the next room, and Lil sat in front of the door that led off the kitchen. She set my plate in front of me and had half a melon for herself.

"There," she said. "All nice and cozy."

"So," Graham began as he ate a piece of bacon, "you wanna spend the next t'ree days stayin' outta sight, or you wanna end this nuisance post-haste?"

"My closets aren't big enough to hide in," I said. "What do you have in mind?"

"Figger we take the fight to Max."

"Oh, see?" Lil pointed her spoon at Graham. "I knew there was a reason I invited you to breakfast."

We began our day at the gym.

Moira was busy accosting two patrons on the far side of the gym for not returning their weights to the proper places when we arrived. I smiled to myself as we walked in. If Max did shoot me in here, Moira would at least give her a solid tongue lashing for cluttering up her gym with my body. Small solace, but it was something.

We worked out for over two hours, alternating between triceps, back, and ab exercises. Graham worked through his reps without conversation. People stole glances at him as he worked, but he didn't seem to notice. His movements were effortless, his breathing slow and methodical. When we finished, he punctuated our mutual quiet with the solitary statement, "That all the weight she's got?"

"Saturday's the day normal people come in here. She has special classes for mutants like you Monday afternoons."

"I work Mondays."

Graham placed the weights back on the stand where he found them. Moira walked by and patted his shoulder.

"It's about time someone picked up after himself," she smiled. "You're a role model to millions."

"Want me t'infuse anybody else here wit' a community spirit?" Graham asked.

"I think I've got it," she said, walking away. "But I'll let you know."

We watched her walk. "She likes you," I said to Graham.

"Who wouldn't?" he shrugged.

We showered up, and Graham brought the car around to the entrance, where I got in.

"You hungry?" he asked.

"Always hungry."

"Me too. Let's go check out what Rudder's has for lunch specials."

I had to laugh. Sitting in plain sight in Lynch's own bar was Graham's answer to getting through the day. Seamus couldn't have us killed in his own establishment, and the simplicity of Graham's idea warmed the heart. Of course we couldn't sit in there forever. It was a short-term solution at best, but it still brought a smile to my face.

It was one thirty in the afternoon when we arrived at Rudder's. Graham dropped me off at the front door before he parked the car, and I went in and took a seat at the bar. Graham followed momentarily and took a seat beside me. It was Saturday afternoon, and, as such, the bar was fuller than it would have been during the week. College kids or families sat two or four to a table eating lunch and enjoying a drink while watching whatever sports happened to be on TV. The bar itself was populated by a mishmash of people, pairs and loners, eating lunch, reading the paper, or just alternating discussions between the bartender and the person next to them. A pleasant hum of conversation encapsulated the entire restaurant, and the steady rhythm of the jukebox seeped in to fill any hanging spots of silence indiscreetly.

All in all, it was a completely restful and enjoyable mood. To be shot in here would add new levels of depth to the definition of the phrase "to suck."

The bartender was a woman with long dirty-blond hair. She wore a pair of ripped blue jeans and a T-shirt with the label "Corona" placed strategically across her breasts. She came over and stood in front of us, smiling at Graham as she did so.

"'Lo, stranger."

"Afternoon, Julia," Graham replied. "Busy?"

"Just starting to pick up," she said. Her eyes were a deep, deep blue. "You know how it is. Hurry up and wait; hurry up and wait." She handed each of us a menu. "I haven't heard from you since our last get-together." She leaned down and crossed her arms on the bar. Her eyes were a deeper shade of blue than ocean coral.

"Sorry, Julia," Graham said. "Meant to give you a call. I've been caught up with this guy last couple days." He pointed his chin at me.

"Kinda glad you didn't," she said, straightening up.

"Mistake?" Graham asked, looking up at her.

"Never a mistake, Graham. With you it's a pleasure, always a pleasure. But it's kind of nice to have the freedom to come and go, too. No strings, nothing awkward. That OK with you?"

"Sure," Graham answered.

"Good." Julia smiled again. "Now what can I get you gentlemen?"

I ordered a tonic water and Graham had a beer. We started off with calamari, and I had the fish and chips for an entrée while Graham ordered a club sandwich. We ate at a leisurely pace, with no intention of leaving our bar stools for the remainder of the afternoon.

We sat and sipped our drinks and watched the first half of a college football game on the overhead television. Around three o'clock Seamus's lackey Charles appeared. He was dressed in an orange sweater with a pink polo shirt underneath, the collar turned up. I pictured him in warmer weather, wearing the sweater draped over his shoulders, the arms tied in a knot in front of him. I pictured someone twisting the arms of the sweater, strangling Charles to death. As I got a clearer vision of the picture, the person strangling Charles turned out to be me. It was not a bad picture.

Charles walked away from the door that led to the stairwell and out onto the bar floor. He surveyed the patrons all around, keeping track, I'm sure, of all the dollars Seamus was laundering through each one of them. As his eyes moved over the crowds, he rested his eyes, for the briefest of moments, on my face. I couldn't be sure because of the distance, but I'm pretty sure he winced. He continued to look through the rest of the crowd, and when he was finished, he walked to the other side of the bar. He greeted two patrons in a friendly manner and then walked back to the stairwell and out of sight, making a concerted effort to not look at Graham or me again.

"That be Charles," Graham said.

"That be. Think he recognized us?"

"Way he so fastidiously avoided eye contact wit' us? Bet my left nut."

"Julia might not take that bet."

"We'll see."

"Think Seamus knows we're here?"

"If he didn't already," Graham said, "he do now. Charlie not likely to touch himself wit'out Seamus's say-so."

"True. Either way, you get points for using the word 'fastidious.'"

"I's been tryin' to build a vocabulary in my spare time."

"You haven't had any spare time lately. You've been too busy working with me."

"Then it just anudder example o' my innate knowledge shinin' through."

Julia circled over to our side of the bar. We ordered another round. She smiled effervescently at Graham and walked away.

"See that smile?" Graham asked. "My night could be gettin' better dramatic'ly later on if I didn't have to babysit you."

"You want me to hurry up and get shot?"

"Depend on what kind o' smile I get when she come back."

Julia returned with our drinks and lingered a moment longer than she needed to, letting her smile cascade over Graham as she placed his beer on the bar.

Graham nodded. "That settles it. We need to take care of dis shit t'night."

"That wasn't a smile; Christ, that was a leer."

"Do things the way I do, sometimes women have trouble restrainin' themselves."

"Good to know."

We endured another hour and a half of sitting on the barstools. The second half of the football game kept us company for a bit and was later replaced by the always-endearing bar trivia TV screen. If this kept up we would soon be reduced to watching the KENO monitor, at which point I would abandon all hopes of Max and simply shoot myself. Thankfully, before it got to that, we were treated to a visit by none other than Seamus Lynch himself.

He was dressed casually in a silk shirt with matching pants and jacket. Every hair was meticulously in place, and he walked with an air of casual arrogance. He smiled congenially at various patrons and motioned to Julia to buy a round for everyone, on the house. A perfect host. An affable, gracious, and bloodthirsty host.

"Gentlemen, gentlemen," Seamus smiled.

He strode up behind the two of us and stood there, hands clasped behind his back, with a stupid, stupid, *stupid* grin on his face.

"This is both a pleasure and an honor," he continued, "having two men of such fine repute dining in my humble little tavern. To what do I owe this tribute, this gesture, of complete and utter…"

"Can it Seamus," Graham interrupted. "Any more shit comes outta you, the short people in here'll be buried alive."

Seamus chuckled. "Always direct, Mr. Porter. There's a lesson to be learned there for me. Very well, let's get straight to the point. Why are you here?"

"You mean aside from the food?"

"We came to see Charles," I said. "It was Graham's turn to make him cry."

Seamus turned his smile towards me. I shifted in my seat to get a better view.

"Don't underestimate Charles, Mr. Miller. That could prove to be most unfortunate."

"I'll keep it in mind." I leaned back against the bar and looked Seamus straight in the eye. "Standing awfully close, aren't you, Seamus? Can't be too careful. Max might aim for my head and accidentally shoot you in the ass."

"Max?" His smile turned into a laugh. "Are you serious? Miller, do you know where you are? There are a dozen people in this building who would make sure you never make it out of here if I so much as snap my fingers. Max is the least of your worries.

"As for you," he turned to Graham, "your chosen loyalties are beginning to register as an annoyance. Continue in this direction, and there's no telling what might happen. Even you, Mr. Porter, can run out of value. Even you can be replaced."

"Doubt it."

Graham's voice had an edge to it that I didn't hear too often. He was irritated. And Graham Porter irritated never boded well for whoever was the source of his irritation. It was akin to playing tag with an angry grizzly bear. From where I was sitting, however, this could only go extremely well for me.

He leaned towards Seamus. "Let's get somethin' straight Lynch," he said. "I could break both yer legs right now and ev'rybody in here would think twice before askin' if you was OK. You know it. I know it. You ain't that tough," he continued, "and you in *my town*. So stop posturin' for the tourists and help us out.

Yer a smart guy. We want the guy shot Stanchion's daughter. Give us that an' call off yer dogs and we're outta here."

"Stanchion's....daughter?" Lynch's grin split his face open wide. "That's what you're after?" His shoulders started to shake as he laughed. "That's what this whole deal has been about? His daughter?"

Lynch stopped laughing, but the smile stayed on his face.

"The two of you parade into my establishment, drop Max's name like you took a hit out on me, and this whole charade is over some little teenage girl?"

His smile was really starting to get on my nerves.

"You sit at my bar and try to throw Max's name in my face? That's good. Miller, do you know how much money it would take to employ Max to kill me? I give Max more business than anyone. You wouldn't even register a glimmer of interest."

"Nobody said we was tryin' t'have you killed," Graham said. "But it no secret Max in an' out a here earlier dis week."

"Lot of people come and go through my doors, Mr. Porter. You included."

"About the girl?" I asked.

Seamus turned to me, grinning savagely.

"Miller, your ignorance is amusing, but it's getting tiresome. You have no clue what type of people you're dealing with. Do you know anything about Michael Stanchion? Anything at all about the people with whom he associates? I assure you, Michael's been intimate with Max in ways in which even he's not aware."

Lynch looked like he was trying not to lick his lips. His smile did not make him an attractive man.

"My enterprise here is so vast, so complex...you have no idea where my hands can reach..."

He really did have a stupid smile.

"And yet you persist in poking around, disrupting my affairs, and now I find out it's because Michael's brat was stupid enough to get shot?"

I'd like him better without the smile.

I wanted that smile off his face.

"I could have you killed instantaneously right now. No need to hire anyone special. Michael learned the dangers of having someone else do your dirty work. That's why his stupid little bitch is lying in the grou—"

I swung off the barstool and punched Seamus in the face. He fell into the table behind him, and the table and Seamus crashed to the ground. He glared up at me from where he landed. His nose and lip were bloody. His smile was gone. I can't say it did anything to improve his appearance.

Graham was on his feet next to me and did a slow turn, making eye contact with every person in the tavern. Nobody moved. Nobody said anything. I took four twenties out of my pocket and put them on the bar for Julia. It left me with five dollars, but I wasn't in the position to ask Graham to ante up right now. I turned and walked towards the exit, and Graham followed behind me. As I pushed open the door to leave, I heard Graham explain my actions to one of the patrons.

"Hair in his lunch. Owner wouldn't take it back. You know how it is."

Seamus Lynch, days earlier

Seamus Lynch watched the rain fall outside his window.

Business was good. Money was pouring in. He was king and his empire was secure. Michael Stanchion had proven to be very useful. Together they had drained Corey Runter of all his funds. There was a verifiable paper trail that could account for all the monies, and Runter had been unable to access any of it. Seamus was king.

He turned away from the window and returned to his desk. Stanchion had served his purpose. He had proven himself loyal, he had proven himself competent, and he had proven himself workable.

But he had also proven himself intelligent.

That was unfortunate. Michael Stanchion was an intelligent man. So intelligent that it wouldn't be long before he realized how much Seamus had been holding out on him or, more importantly, how much more he was more or less entitled to get. That's the problem with intelligent people. Give them a little power and a little money, and they immediately see ways to achieve more.

No, Michael Stanchion's usefulness might have run its course. The election was in mid-November. If Stanchion were to be strategically removed right before the election, it would plunge the state into a bit of chaos. The current governor was a fool, and Seamus had flourished under his lazy eyes. It would take almost no effort to continue to do so.

Yes, it was time to get rid of Michael Stanchion.

Runter would have been perfect for that. Without money he would not have been able to pay his girls, his guns, or his outstanding debts. His world would have come crashing down around him.

He would have been very angry when that happened. He would have wanted to take his anger out on somebody. Seemed like a good idea to Seamus to beat Runter to the punch. A well-placed phone call could've cranked up Runter's suspicions about his money. A well-placed phone call could've pointed him in the direction of Michael Stanchion.

Runter was emotional. It was so easy to push his buttons. He would've taken out Stanchion without even realizing how futile it was. All of Runter's monies were in Stanchion's name. All of the money was completely unavailable to Runter.

Runter takes out Stanchion, and Seamus has already disabled Runter. Michael Stanchion is dead; Corey Runter is useless, Seamus is king. It all had a nice ring to it.

Of course that all changed when Runter got himself killed. Stupid. He tried to take things into his own hands. There wasn't a person in Rhode Island who would follow his orders. He had no place here. Lynch's men were loyal to Lynch, and most of them were scared of Porter. That was a no-win situation from the start.

No-win for Runter, but it was fine with Seamus. Runter took himself out of the picture and Lynch didn't have to lift a finger. Now all he had to deal with was Stanchion. Of course, with Runter gone, he would have to go to Plan B. Runter killing Stanchion would've been easy and cheap. Plan B meant Max. Max was expensive. But, you get what you pay for, and Max had already proven to be professional. One phone call would put everything in motion.

Seamus swiveled in his chair and looked back out the window at the driving rain. Everything always came together. Everything always fell right into place. He watched the rain until it was too dark to see. Then he swiveled back around to his desk and reached for the phone.

It was good to be king.

"You got issues."

We were in the Mustang cruising up to Route 1.

"You want to list them?" I asked.

"Ain't enough time. Beginnin' t'think you a bit suicidal, though, way you punched Seamus. Funny, but suicidal."

"Seamus didn't seem to be too cognizant of ordering a hit on me."

"Sure," Graham answered. "'Course, wit' Seamus bein' one hunnert percent criminal, dere is the slight possibility he might not be completely truthful."

"Got nothing to do with truth," I said. "You said it yourself. He was posturing. He was taunting us about Stanchion and Stanchion's daughter. Bastard was enjoying it, too. But he wasn't concerned with us."

"So what, he just come over to buy us a drink?"

"He came over to acknowledge we were in his bar. But he wasn't there to tear us down, or make a run at us, or say good-bye before we got shot."

"Maybe he just dumb."

"There is that."

"You thinkin' Seamus ain't that distressed about us?" Graham asked.

"Embarrassing, but possible."

"Wow," Graham said. "He is dumb."

"Considerably."

Graham thought a moment. "So who is he concerned wit'?"

"I'm thinking Stanchion's in this much deeper than he's letting on."

"Stanchion?"

"I'd bet your left nut."

"Bet's already been taken. Why Stanchion?"

"Just a hunch."

"Oh, good. At least we got somethin' concrete t'work with."

"You heard him," I said. "He had nothing but contempt for Stanchion and his daughter. Man like Lynch'll use Stanchion for whatever he needs, but there always comes a time to get rid of him."

"I see. You think that time is now?"

"I think it's close."

"Stanchion home yet?"

"He's throwing a party in Newport tonight."

"We on the guest list?"

"Courtesy of Lil."

"Girl comes in handy. We goin' t'see Stanchion now?"

"Yep."

Graham rolled his shoulders. "We doin' an awful lotta runnin' around on your hunches." He blew out some air. "If Max is followin' us, she gettin' a workout."

"I'm hoping to tire her out. Maybe her aim won't be so hot."

"Ev'ry little bit helps, buddy," Graham said. "Ev'ry little bit helps."

Jessica checked herself in the mirror one more time.

She wanted everything to be perfect. Hair, makeup, clothes, everything. Perfect. She pulled her hair back and held it in place with a silver hair clip, a sweet-sixteen birthday gift from her grandmother. Very carefully she applied eye shadow and mascara. She touched up her lipstick and admired herself in the full-length mirror on her door. Her sweater was Tommy's favorite color, and her skirt and heels made her look older. She liked that. She should look older tonight.

She took a deep breath. She could almost hear her heart beating in her breast. She was nervous, excited, scared, and couldn't wait to see Tommy. She was going to make him so happy. Tommy had been so patient. The other girls had talked of sex; some of them had shared stories of their experiences. Jessica knew she and Tommy were going to be together forever. It was time for the two of them to move to the next level too. Her heart beat faster. Sharing herself with him was going to be so special. So wonderful.

Her parents were in Newport at a very important convention for her father. Her mother had told her they probably wouldn't be home until late, and she had already called her mother and told her she was going to bed early. Jessica walked out the front door into the darkness of her front yard. The moon hung low behind the trees to her right. Her parents had both gone in her father's car. She had the keys to her mother's. She turned over the engine, turned on the lights, and headed over to Tommy's.

Tommy's parents were gone for the weekend. He had the house to himself. He had told Jessica he was spending the night studying and would call her tomorrow. Wouldn't he be surprised when she showed up at his house! She smiled to herself as she drove. They would have the house to themselves. They could crawl into bed together, make love, and then hold each other tight under the covers. The knots in her stomach got tighter. She bit her lower lip and her smile spread across her face.

Tommy's house was dark except for one upstairs window. The room glowed where he was studying. Jessica smiled to herself in the darkness as she imagined his surprise. She parked the car on the street and got out. She smoothed her skirt and walked to the front door. She knocked lightly. Tommy didn't answer so she knocked again. Still no answer. Jessica twisted the knob and opened the door. The house was quiet and empty. She liked the feeling. It was like the house was theirs.

She switched on the hall light and walked up the stairs. Slowly, one step at a time. She had worn the heels for a reason. They were adults. They should act like it. They would act like it. No need to rush. She reached the top of the stairs and turned towards Tommy's room. The door was shut. She ran her fingers through her hair and fixed her sweater. She took a deep breath and opened the door.

"Tommy!" she called.

But Tommy was not studying. He was in bed already. And a woman was with him. She had blond hair and she was naked and she...

"Ms. Hurdtz?" Jessica stammered.

"Jess?! What the fuck!" Tommy cried.

"Oh my God," she heard Ms. Hurdtz say.

Jessica turned and ran down the hallway and back down the stairs. She didn't look back. She couldn't see if she wanted to; her eyes were full of tears. Shame, hurt, pain, anger all came crashing down as she threw herself into her mother's car. She wanted to get away; she wanted to go far, far away and bury her head and never see anyone again in her life.

She wanted to die.

She did not feel grown up anymore. She felt like a little, little girl. She didn't want to go home. She didn't want to be alone. She wanted someone who made sense. She wanted someone who would help her make sense. She wanted her mother.

She pulled out into traffic and tried to control her sobs. Her parents were at a convention in Newport. She remembered her father saying it was on the beach. Jessica wanted her mother. Her mother would hold her and make everything all right.

She headed north up the highway and took the exit for Newport. A convention on the beach couldn't be that hard to find. She turned off the radio and drove in silence. By the time she was driving over the Newport Bridge, her cheeks were still damp with her tears, but she had stopped crying.

She crossed the bridge, passed the graveyard, and drove right into the heart of Newport on America's Cup Avenue. Even though the summer season was over, people still jammed the sidewalks on a Saturday night. She slowed down as throngs of people crossed the street, heading away from the hotels and into the clubs. She snaked along the road, passed the Red Parrot, and drove up a steep hill. She crossed over Bellevue Avenue and down the hill towards the beach. Her parents had taken her here last summer for lunch. It looked different in the dark on a Saturday night; bright lights, noise, more cars, more people.

The beach stretched out over to her right, a long flat stretch of land. The beach was different than Bellevue. The noise, the people were all gone. She drove the entire length and found the club tucked away in the corner at the end of the beach. She parked her car in the lot and hurried to the front door. The door opened before she even got there, and a large man in a suit put his hand up and stopped her.

"Just one moment, Miss," the man said. "Where do you think you're going, please?"

"My mother," Jessica started. "I need to see—"

"This is a private function, Miss," the man interrupted. "Not a high school dance." He looked at her in the glare of the spotlight over the door. "Why don't you go home, clean yourself up, and have your boyfriend take you out for an ice cream sundae. The grown-ups have work to do in here."

He shut the door in her face. Jessica stood there stunned, shivering in the cold. The tears returned, hot and burning down her face. Humiliation, pain, and despair returned to her in droves. She turned and walked away, away from the club, past the car, out of the parking lot, and onto the beach. She didn't know where to go. She just hugged herself in the night air and began walking down the long, lonely stretch of beach.

—61—

Michael Stanchion smiled and ushered the final guests into the reception. He was nervous. Everything had to go right tonight. There were so many variables, so many things he could not control. One mistake and everything could go to hell. Everything he'd worked for and planned for could go to hell in the span of the next six hours.

Both Vanessa and Erin were here tonight. Erin was smart enough to stay away from him while his wife was here, and that would explain why he was distancing himself from her. He'd left instructions for Max through Mulligan's. At nine p.m. sharp, there would be a lone blond woman walking the beach. That was the target Max needed to take out.

The debate between Michael and the current governor was scheduled to begin at seven. Public debates almost never occurred in this political arena, but this had been another one of Erin's public relation gems. Michael had to agree it was an excellent idea. He truly was going to miss her.

A late dinner was scheduled for nine, assuring everyone the debate would not exceed two hours. Michael had told Erin to meet him on the beach at nine so that they could spend a little time together away from his wife. The ruse worked almost too easily. Erin agreed immediately. She was overly eager to get to the beach and wait for him. She seemed to light up once he suggested it. The poor dear. She really was head over heels for him.

Of course, Michael would never meet her on the beach. He would be enjoying a fine dinner with his wife, surrounded by some of the most powerful leaders in the state. Erin, meanwhile, would be having her brains blown out down by the water. It was a shame. He truly was going to miss her. But what could he do?

Politics were politics.

Erin nestled herself behind two large shrubs amidst the rocks at the far end of the beach. She had more room than she needed. Her trench coat had allowed her to carry her rifle with ease, and Michael had given her a reason to leave early before she had to come up with one herself.

The darkness of the night gave her perfect cover. The moon hung low over the ocean to her right, and the streetlights glowed softly down to her left. No one could see her tucked away up on the rocks. She fit a silencer to her rifle. She had brought night goggles, but she didn't really need them. While she stayed hidden, the streetlights gave enough light to see anyone walking along the beach.

A lone blond walking the beach....For a brief moment she entertained the notion that Michael had hired Max with the intention of killing Erin. Wouldn't that be the height of irony? Perhaps he just wanted Erin here to discover the body with him as a witness. All those thoughts were quickly discarded as she saw a young woman walking by herself down along the water. She carried a pair of heels and hugged herself as she walked. Erin caught the glow of her long blond hair in the moonlight. She checked her watch. 9:02.

Erin studied the woman's face through the scope of her rifle. Pretty young thing. A shame... She squeezed off two rounds from her rifle. The woman's body fell to the ground.

Like shooting ducks in a barrel...

I've had the pleasure of seeing the band the Dropkick Murphys live in concert twice in my life. They are a band from Boston that blends punk music with Irish music and puts on a thoroughly riotous show. Seeing as how a good majority of people from Boston are, indeed, Irish punks themselves, one could easily call the Murphys a hometown band.

Now I joke, but one of the aspects that is so refreshing about this band is the fact that it is comprised of blue-collar workers who just happen to be able to play instruments. You can see it in their mannerisms and attitudes, hear it in their lyrics, and watch it in the crowd they attract: The Dropkick Murphys are simply good, hardworking people who have the added bonus of being able to play kickass music. I saw them play on St. Patrick's Day in Boston once, and the pride that emanated from the stage was almost tangible.

Newport, Rhode Island, has a different feel to it. It tastes of money, and entitlement, and high society. The Murphys earn your respect. Newport insists upon it.

Graham and I were headed to Newport. I had the Murphys cranked in the car as we drove over the bridge. It's good to remember your roots. The band made me feel at ease. I had trouble feeling comfortable in a town that housed mansions that were originally built to be used as summer homes for only three months out of the year.

The Newport Bridge lit up brilliantly against the encroaching dusk as we crossed over the water that separated Newport from the rest of the state. Some historians will tell you that Newport and the rest of Aquidneck Island is the actual, legal state of Rhode Island, and the rest of the state is just an add-on. I was pretty sure that theory was proposed by a prominent member of the Newport community.

The city is famous for the mansions that line Bellevue Avenue. These structures epitomize the raw affluence that has come to be associated with Newport, Rhode Island, although anyone who ventures three streets further comes in contact with a much different view of the social structures that reside in town. Still, the mansions are the figurehead for the town, perpetuating a lifestyle and elegance that caters to whoever wants to take part in it. Or whoever can afford to.

Because of this, the mansions are rented out for various functions, usually aligning with an individual who wants to proclaim some sort of mastery over the rest of the human race, or at least feel as though he or she is above the masses for a few hours. Michael Stanchion was one of these people.

Stanchion was holding court tonight at the mansion named the Birches, thus named because of two giant birch trees that flanked either side of the outer driveway. We turned off the street and started down the quarter-mile entranceway. Past the birch trees, streetlights built to resemble old-fashioned gas lamps were erected to guide you as you traveled to the manor.

"You ever been here before?" Graham asked.

"Nope," I answered. "You?"

"You serious?"

"Hardly ever. According to Lil, Stanchion loves Newport. Held another reception here in town the beginning of last month."

"Lil told you that?"

"She did."

Graham snorted. "Sammy, you ever think maybe since yer the detective, it might be appropriate fer you t'do some o' the detectin'?"

"Not when I surround myself with such capable people."

The driveway was made of crushed stone, and there was a large space for parking off to the side. We avoided the valet and pulled into an empty space. The front of the mansion glowed brightly. Inside lights lit every window, and outside lights illuminated the entire edifice as well as the surrounding grounds. As we got out of the car, we could hear a steady stream of voices coming from around the back of the house.

"More'n one party going on," Graham observed.

"Uh-huh. Lil said Stanchion's around back, in the garden."

"Outside? It's fuckin' November."

"Inside was already booked. They had the caterers put up tenting and bring in heaters. Michael's either extremely popular or has more pull than I want to admit."

"Prob'ly a little bit of both."

We took a minute to get acquainted with our surroundings. There was only one way in and out, the drive down which we came. All of the cars were parked off to the side. The Birches mansion stood in the center of the property, with a wide expanse of front and back yard, both of which were saturated with electric light. Around the border of the property, lost in the darkness, was a thin expanse of woodland.

"Tough to sneak around," I said. "Whole place is lit up."

"Yep," Graham agreed. "We get tagged, more'n likely we getting' tagged from above. Stay away from the trees and close to the building. Place is bright, but we're dealin' wit' a professional. And where there's a will...."

Graham stopped in his tracks and looked to his left. I followed his gaze. Two cars away from ours was a gold Karmann Ghia convertible.

"Max got here before us?" I asked. "She psychic?"

Graham felt the hood of the car.

"Engine's still warm. She just got here." He scanned the grounds. He pointed to the far wall across the yard. A small cluster of trees formed a wall between the Birches and its neighboring mansion. "There ya go, buddy. Fire escape."

I looked in the direction Graham was pointing. In between the trees and the mansion, right on the fringe of the lights illuminating the outside, a figure was scurrying up the fire escape. Slung over the figure's right shoulder was what appeared to be a rifle.

"She's heading for the roof," I said.

"Really?" Graham asked.

"Might have to go with the option that she's not here to shoot me."

"Detective skills startin' t'shine through," Graham responded. "'Course, dat means I've wasted my entire day hangin' wit' you."

"She's here to shoot somebody, Graham."

Graham nodded. "Would be the reason for the gun."

"Probably something we'd best prevent."

"Prob'ly. Depend on who she's here to shoot."

There was another fire escape on the near side of the mansion, on the wall closest to us. I started towards it, and Graham made for the back of the house. The plan was for him to alert the party to the imminent danger while I attempted to dissuade Max from shooting anyone. Somehow I thought Graham got the better end of the deal.

The fire escape ended halfway down the first floor of the manor. I jumped up, grabbed the bottom rung, and pulled myself up. The rungs were cold, and flecks of rust came off in my hands as I climbed. From below, I could hear the classical music setting the tone for the party. It sounded like Emma Cole, who was a phenomenal pianist, and the only one to whom I would actually give pause and listen.

Given our history, I was in no particular hurry to prevent Michael Stanchion from being shot. From what I had learned of him and his campaign, his death would only improve the state, and I was pretty sure Graham would agree. But there was always the possibility that Max would fire at someone else, and with the crowds of people below, Lil being one of them, we couldn't in good conscience turn and walk away.

Spotlights were affixed all along the top walls, and as I climbed upwards I got lost in their brilliance. I climbed the last third of the fire escape in blindness from the lighting, which did not bode well, seeing as how I was meeting a killer on the roof. I made it past the spotlights and to the top of the roof, praying my eyes would adjust before I got my head blown off.

I climbed the last two rungs and poked my head over the top of the roof. While my eyes adjusted to the darkness, I felt out in front of me to get my bearings. A small stone wall about a foot high and six inches wide formed a border around the roof. I pulled myself over it and let myself down on the roof itself.

The roof was flat and made out of an asphalt-like tar. My feet crunched on it as I touched down. Mini-spotlights the size of house bulbs were embedded in the wall encircling the roof and gave off little halos of light every twenty feet or so. The entire roof was the size of a small parking lot. I could see a giant rooster-shaped weathervane towards the center, and in front of me was a patch of roughed-up gravel that looked as if it was used to cover a hole where a chimney had been.

I pulled my gun out and scanned the roof. The backyard was lit up for Stanchion's party, and the lights glowed against the back wall. Across the way I caught Maxine's silhouette against the lighting. She was kneeling down behind the wall, her rifle leaning against it, wrapping a pair of night goggles around her head. Her hair was pulled back in a ponytail, and she was dressed in form-fitting black. The lights provided the perfect backdrop against which to view her figure, which was honestly the nicest I'd ever seen on an assassin.

If I had the right, I would have whistled.

"Michael's been intimate with Max in ways in which even he's not aware," Seamus had said. Michael, you hound. I wondered if he'd take it personally that his former girlfriend was here to put a bullet through his head. That alone did not speak highly of their relationship, but counseling was probably a moot issue at this point.

Intimate in ways even he wasn't aware...there was more to that statement. What was it? Hell, Max was right here. Maybe she'd entertain a brief Q&A before she opened fire. Sell the story rights to Hollywood; we both retire rich. I took a deep breath and started across the roof. There was no way this was going to go well.

She picked up her rifle and sighted through the scope. She moved with the sureness of a jungle predator; there was no tenseness, no hurry. I held my gun and ran towards her. There was no time to be patient. My feet slid across some loose gravel. Even with the party below us, I knew she heard me before she turned. She was, as Graham had said, the consummate professional.

She was fluid in her motion. Before I could bring my gun down on her, she had her rifle gripped by the barrel and swung it around at my legs. She took my feet out from under me with her gun, and I went skidding down on the roof, my gun clattering away from me. By the time I regained my footing, she was back against the ledge, calmly sighting through the scope.

The party was in full swing below us, but the two of us were locked in an echoing silence. Nothing existed save for the two of us. Time seemed to freeze. Against the lights I saw her finger start to press down on the trigger. My own gun was lost in the darkness. I threw myself at her right shoulder, where she rested the butt of her rifle. I hit her just as the shot exploded from the gun. A flash of light erupted against the darkness of the roof, and a cannon went off in my ears.

Below us I heard a woman's scream get cut short.

Lil?

We tumbled across the rooftop in the darkness. Max drove her fist into the bridge of my nose. A sharp stab of pain bit into my eyes, and a well of blood started to pour from the center of my face. I was flat on my back. Max was on top of me, straddling me at the waist. Her figure looked even better up close. A small voice in the back of my head told me to enjoy what I could.

From the party below, I heard a woman yell, "One of ye feckin' morons give me a hand with this woman! She's hurt! Michael! Let go of your dick and call a feckin' ambulance!"

Lil was alive.

Max punched me hard twice in the same spot where Corey Runter had opened me with a screwdriver days earlier. Her pinpoint knowledge of where to hit assured me that Corey had either given her a detailed description of what he'd done or had asked her for pointers. My body wanted to curl up in the fetal position. Max stayed on top of me and prevented that from happening, keeping my body stretched out and basically inviting paralysis.

The small voice in the back of my head was losing credibility very quickly.

I heard the clamor dying down at the party. Max hovered over me and slowly brought her face down to mine.

"I could kill you in nine different ways right now," she whispered into my left ear. "I want you to know the only reason I'm letting you live is so you will forever be wondering when I'll come back. You will spend the rest of your life looking over your shoulder." She licked my ear, lingering on my earlobe. "Have fun."

I felt her rise off my body, and then she was gone. I didn't even hear her leave.

I lay on my back and stared at the night sky.

"I'm looking forward to our second date," I mumbled into the darkness. "So glad I made an impression."

"You look worse ev'ry time I see you."

Graham met me at the base of the fire escape.

"Y'need help walkin', or y'still remember how t'do that?"

"I can manage," I said. I looked across the lawn to where the ambulance was closing its doors. "Fill me in. What happened down here?"

"Stanchion's wife got shot 'stead o' Stanchion. She wuz standin' right next t'him over there," Graham pointed. "Shot went off an' punctured her lung. Sloppy shot, but it did the job. She chokin' on blood bubbles while she dyin'. Ambulance takin' her in for the official autopsy now." He paused. "What were you doin' up there?"

"Wrestling Max."

"Uh-huh." He watched the ambulance pass us. "You did a shitty job."

The night air was cold in its stillness. "Did the best I could," I said.

Graham looked at me and studied my face. "Was me," he said, "she wouldn'ta got the shot off."

We walked in silence across the grounds to where the tent was set up in back of the mansion. Space heaters erected an instant wall of heat once you were back there, but despite the crowd of people, the silence got louder once we reached the party. People stood around, empty glasses in hand, looking aimlessly for a reason to remain. The party was over. It was bad form to leave Stanchion in his grief, but most of the guests didn't know him well enough to offer any close counsel. Lil spotted us and strode over.

"...lets his wife get shot instead o' him, and then stands there an' pretends t'grieve," she was saying to absolutely no one. "Feckin' coward, he is. He's over there by himself," she said to me, pointing over her shoulder. "Now would be the best time for you to go shoot him." She continued to walk past us. "If I go see him right now, I'll strangle 'im with me bare hands. Wouldn't be a loss at all, I'll tell ye that. O'course yer friend Lieutenant Simon would 'ave words with me, but she just doesn't like me. Probably because she knows I..."

She walked out of earshot, but I was sure this was a conversation that would carry on well into the night. Probably regardless of whether I was around or not.

"Girl means business."

"One of us should," Graham answered. He looked past me towards Stanchion. "You gonna take care of this?"

"Yep."

"Want a hand?"

"Nope."

He stood next to me a moment, the embodiment of calm. Graham was always calm. Serenity personified.

"I'll wait for you at the car."

I nodded.

"Good luck to ya."

Michael stood by himself at the edge of the tenting. The crowd had gathered at a respectful distance from him, waiting to see if he needed anything or wanted to be left alone, at which point they could go home. I passed through the crowd towards Stanchion, and the people eagerly moved aside for me. The wound in my side was reopened and my shirt was damp with fresh blood. My face was a mess and my nose was probably broken. This was beginning to become my evening look for upscale parties. Maybe I'd start a trend.

Michael wasn't crying, but his body was shaking as I approached him. I put my hand on his shoulder.

"Michael—" I began.

"...again," Michael was stammering. "It happened again. It happened again."

"Let's go for a walk, Michael," I said, guiding him out the tent and away from the house. The spotlights lit up the backyard as brightly as the front, and we walked quietly across the space. I could almost hear a collective sigh of relief as Michael left the party. All the concerned citizens could go home now guilt-free.

Michael and I stopped at the edge of the light encircling the property. I waited. Michael stared at the trees just beyond the light. Finally he spoke.

"Just like before," he whispered.

"What do you mean, just like before?"

"Another one. Another one dead. Jessica. My wife." He paused. The generator hummed behind us, back up at the tent. I let him continue. "I'm done. These people...they won't stop. They won't...I'm done." He looked over at me. His gaze was heavy. "It was Max, wasn't it?"

I nodded. "It was."

He nodded to himself, as if confirming something. "That bastard Seamus. Using Max to get at me. His idea of irony. A fucking joke."

"You and Seamus have a falling out?" He was talking. Keep him going.

"We could have worked together. That night you saw me in the bar...he was using me to double-cross Runter. With Runter gone, I thought we'd be fine. Fifty-fifty. But...you tried...you tried to warn me."

"What happened?"

"What always happens?" His voice was tiny. "Money. It came down to money. And now...Vanessa...and Jessica..."

"Don't forget Aaron."

He looked at me. His eyes were empty. "Vanessa said you talked with him." He opened his mouth and shut it. He shook his head. "Fucking Seamus."

"You don't seem surprised he hired Max to get you."

Michael's mouth contorted into what I thought at first was a small smile, but then I noticed the tears coming down his face.

"He thought it was funny. I had hired Max to do a job, and it blew up in my face. He—"

"You hired Max to kill Seamus? Are you kidding?"

"No." His voice caught on a sob. "I hired...Max...I hired Max to kill this woman Erin who I thought could sabotage my campaign. But..."

"Erin and Max are the same person," I cut in.

"She was supposed to shoot Erin on the beach...just get rid of her." His voice was shaky. "I'd never do it again. I didn't want to compromise my campaign. I didn't want anything traceable. I never used names. I just gave a description. A blond woman. Alone on the beach. But Erin and Max...Max and Erin..."

All the pieces fell into place.

Stanchion's voice trailed off. I finished his thoughts for him.

"A blond woman did get shot on the beach." I took a breath. "Max shot your daughter."

He nodded. His body was convulsing as he sobbed.

"And you knew."

"I...f-found her b...body on the beach..."

"And then you came to me."

He clutched my sleeve and buried his head in my shoulder as he wept. I jerked my arm back and shook him off.

"And then what, Mike?" I asked as he stumbled. "Did you hope I'd find Max? Take care of her for you? Bury your secret?"

Stanchion stood there, head bent, shoulders bowed. His body shook in spasms of his sorrow and guilt. His mouth was open in a twisted show of pain, but there was no sound. His demons were out. He was vulnerable right now. The wrong words could push him over the edge, make him desperate, irrational. In crisis interventions such as this, one has to make sure to choose one's words with great care.

"You are a disgusting human being," I said.

The proper thing to do would be to get him to the authorities. They'd lock him up. Some would fight to get him counseling. Rehabilitate him. Make him a productive member of society. Everyone deserves a second chance, right?

I thought about Jessica's opportunities for a second chance. I thought about Vanessa's.

Stanchion had fallen to his knees. His whole body shook. He held his face in his hands. He was in a very fragile state of mind.

"Do you remember when you hired me, Mike?" I asked. "You remember what you asked me to do?"

Stanchion's breathing was coming in erratic gulps of air. He wrapped his arms around his head and doubled over on the ground.

"You asked me to find your daughter's killer and then kill him," I said. "I've been kicked off this case. But I'll meet you halfway. I've found your daughter's killer."

I dropped my gun on the ground next to him.

"I'll let you do the rest."

I turned and walked away from Michael Stanchion.

I was halfway back to the tent when I heard the gunshot.

I didn't even turn around to look at the body.

We were standing around Lil's Jeep.

I had returned to the Mustang to find all four of my tires neatly shot out. Max's way of saying goodbye. I promptly called my insurance agent, Bob Botelho in Warwick (the only insurance agent who not only had no reservations insuring me, but who also could be reached at his office at 11:30 at night), who informed me that while bullets were not normally covered under typical roadside damage, he'd make some phone calls and see what he could do.

Lucille Simon broke away from the group of Newport police officers and came over to us.

"Here's your gun," she said, dropping it in my hand.

"Thanks. He wrestled it away from me."

"I'm sure you put up a fight." She didn't make eye contact with me.

"So how'd you get out here? Newport's not your jurisdiction."

"Vanessa and Michael are both Narragansett residents. When I got the call on the second death, I came out here as a courtesy. When I heard your name come over the radio, I almost turned around and went home."

"Courteous," Lil smiled.

Most of the people had left by now. A few had stayed around to watch the new developments and see if they could get their picture in the paper. The police had cordoned off the crime scene, and all the yellow tape made the Birches look like a yuppie Alcatraz.

"I've spoken with the police, Lucille," I said. "The guests backed up my story. We're not needed anymore. If it's all right with you, we're gonna take off."

"Actually, Sam, the police are going to want to—"

"Lucille, we're going home," Lil said flatly.

Lucille met Lil's gaze and then looked away. "I know how to reach you if I need anything else," she said, and turned and walked back across the grounds.

"Direct," I said.

"I'm tired Samuel. And aggravated. You want to argue with me?"

"Not on your life." I climbed in the passenger seat of Lil's Jeep. "What happened to Graham?"

"I told him to go home. Police and Graham don't mix." She drove down the driveway and turned left on Bellevue Avenue. "I offered him a ride, but he said he knew someone down on the wharf, and he'd crash there. Said he'd find a ride home in the morning."

America's Cup Avenue was lit up and empty as we drove down. The bars were still open, but without the tourists, there wasn't much foot traffic out this late. It was pleasant. Lil passed through the downtown at a fairly normal pace and then hurtled her Jeep over the Newport Bridge. She gave two bucks to the toll-booth attendant and crossed to the other side.

"So what happened with Michael?"

"Shot himself in the head."

"He did. You have anything to do with that?"

"I encouraged him."

"Don't blame you. Was there any particular reason?"

One of the things I liked about Lil was she didn't press me. She let things come out naturally. Everything was matter-of-fact. One of the reasons I could tell her the truth was because she could deal with it. Another reason was because she let me. She never made me feel like I had to tell her what she wanted to hear.

"He's responsible for his daughter's death. Ordered a hit on his mistress, gave a blank description to save his rep, and got his signals crossed. Killed his daughter. Coward found out what happened and stuck his head in the sand. Tried to hide."

"And before that he sent his son to prison."

"And then his wife gets shot with a bullet meant for him, if you're keeping score."

Lil glanced sideways at me as she drove. "Max is supposed to be the best shooter around. Rooftop with a clear view? How does she flub up that shot?"

"I gave her a hand."

The highway merged into Boston Neck Road. As we drove, police cars sat parked at various points, patiently waiting for Saturday night drunks to pass by. Lil slowed down to a respectable speed and waited for me to continue.

"Graham met me after Vanessa got shot. Said if it was him up there, Max never would've gotten the shot off."

"Graham's probably right. Graham also got stonewalled by five of Stanchion's personal security goons long enough for Vanessa to get dead. Life's not perfect. Did Graham's comments have any influence over the way you handled Michael?"

"A bit," I said.

"Live your life looking for someone else's approval, babe, it ain't your life anymore."

"Stanchion was a slug," I said. "The world is not going to mourn his passing."

"Big picture? You're absolutely right. The man was a creep. He deserved to die. And you helped him. I applaud you for that. What you've got to reconcile for yourself is your reason for doing it. Did you hand him your gun because of what he did to his family, or because Graham made you feel incompetent? Were you trying to reconcile for what you saw as a failure on your part?"

"End justifies the means here, Lil. Dead is dead. The man is gone. Scales are balanced. You said yourself he deserved it."

"The reasons are important too, Samuel. The why is very important. You still have to look at yourself in the mirror every morning."

I closed my eyes and thought about Jessica Stanchion. I was pretty sure my reflection would be crystal clear tomorrow.

Lil dropped me off at my house, promising to see me tomorrow. She'd offered to stay the night, but I'd be lousy company to anyone tonight, even her. AAA would have my car towed home by morning, but even then I still needed four new tires. So for the time being I had the solace of being a prisoner in my own home. For the moment it was nice to have a decision made for me that was out of my control.

It was one in the morning, but I was nowhere near tired. I poured myself a glass of Jameson's and sat and stared at it for the better part of half an hour. Lil had asked the question that I was trying to ignore myself. I told myself that Stanchion deserved to die. He did. But did I goad him into killing himself because I was feeling useless and trying to play catch-up for my failure on the roof? Or did I give him my gun with Jessica's redemption in mind? Did it matter?

Yeah, it did.

Lil had a point. The why is important. The motivation is what validates the action. Killing Stanchion because he killed his daughter was justifiable. Killing Stanchion because I screwed up was an excuse. There have to be rules. Even if you set them yourself, there have to be rules. You need to be able to hold yourself accountable. Otherwise you're outside the loop. Above the law. Playing God. And once you're outside the loop, you've got no right coming back in.

I tossed it back and forth in my head. I did the right thing killing Stanchion. I wouldn't take it back if I could. But the reasons were important. I was reacting out of anger. Anger for Jessica? Anger at myself?

I let it bounce back and forth until I decided it was too big an issue for me to solve. Life isn't perfect, Lil had said. Neither was I. I drained my glass in one swallow, got off the couch, and called the prison in Cranston to tell Aaron Stanchion that he was now an orphan.

Lil had made chili and brought it over to share for dinner. I loved chili. I loved Lil's company. Hence, I chose never to learn how to make chili myself.

"A little tired, are we?" she asked as she placed a grocery bag on the counter.

"It's Sunday," I answered. "Little Steven."

Little Steven's Underground Garage was a syndicated radio program one of the local stations ran on Sunday mornings. It lived up to its hype of the "coolest radio show on the planet," but it also ran at eight a.m. I didn't fall asleep until six in the morning. I awoke at eight. It was now three in the afternoon. You do the math.

Lil placed two plates on the breakfast table that stood in the corner of my kitchen. "If your house was burning down, and you only had time to grab three things before you had to get out, what would you take?"

"My car keys, my jacket, and my sunglasses," I said, bringing a loaf of Irish soda bread over.

"Well that's not a fair question for you."

"Why not?"

"That's all you own."

I handed her a glass of wine and poured myself a glass of water from the sink.

"Am I drinking alone?"

"I'll sit right next to you."

I scooped out two bowlfuls of chili and placed them on the plates. As my breakfast table also served as my lunch table and my dinner table, I figured if I was neat, I wouldn't have to set my table for breakfast tomorrow.

"What about you?"

"What about me?"

"What would you take?"

"Well it's not a fair question for me either."

"Of course."

"First of all, my house would never be burning down. I have too many nice things inside, and I would never be able to choose just three things."

"Of course."

"Second of all, the boys at the fire department are always smiling at me when I walk by. They're extremely nice and I'm sure they would be there in a moment's notice if indeed my house were to catch on fire, and extinguish the fire immediately."

"There's probably a couple there round the clock hiding in the bushes, peering in your bedroom window."

"Hush."

"Of course."

"Thirdly, if, God forbid, I did have to vacate my home and forgo my belongings, I know exactly what I would grab. I'd take that photo Everett took of you and me sitting in the corner booth after opening night was over at our bar in Philadelphia."

I knew the picture. Opening night had been wonderfully busy. We'd run our asses off. I remember collapsing in the booth at two a.m. thinking about all the cleanup we still had to do and then coming back and doing the whole thing again tomorrow. Lil had sat down in the booth beside me and rested her head on my shoulder. Everett had been taking pictures all night long, and the camera was still in his hand. He snapped the picture before Lil showed him her middle finger. I was impressed he was that quick.

I smiled. "Place was trashed."

"And we were exhausted. I like that shot. It was the very first time we did something together that was productive."

"Don't you count—"

"I said productive."

I took a drink of water. "What brought this conversation on? You plan on paring down your possessions?"

"I've been thinking about the dead girl in your case."

"Jessica."

"Jessica. And how she'll never be able to dream of a future, and chase those dreams, and succeed and fail and everything else. It makes you look at your own life."

"You have a good life?"

"I have a good life."

She took a sip of her wine.

"I have a better life because of you."

She placed her glass down on the table and looked at me.

"I love you very much, Samuel."

"I love you too."

"Hush. Eat your meal."

"Of course."

About the Author

Marc Blevins is the author of the previous Samuel Miller novel, **Hard Sell**. He lives in Rhode Island. Feel free to contact him at SamuelMiller1@cox.net.

Printed in the United States
69766LV00005B/88